Lock Down Publications and Ca$h
Presents

I0658222

THESE
VICIOUS STREETS
Love & Money

By
Gritty and Raw Crime Novelist
Prince A. Tauhid

First Edition 2023

Printed in the United States of America

This is a work of fiction. Names, characters, places, and incidents either are products of the author's imagination or are used fictitiously. Any similarity to actual events or locales or persons, living or dead, is entirely coincidental.

Lock Down Publications
P.O. Box 944
Stockbridge, GA 30281
www.lockdownpublications.com

Like our page on Facebook: Lock Down Publications
www.facebook.com/lockdownpublications.ldp

Stay Connected with Us!

Text **LOCKDOWN** to 22828 to stay up-to-date with new releases, sneak peaks, contests and more…

Like our page on Facebook:
Lock Down Publications

Join Lock Down Publications/The New Era Reading Group

Visit our website:
www.lockdownpublications.com

Follow us on Instagram:
Lock Down Publications

Email Us: We want to hear from you!

PROLOGUE

The day her world fell apart was the moment Carmen Jenine Margaux (pronounced Mar-go) was approached by the FBI (DEA agents) upon her visit to the gynecologist for a follow-up. Prior to, Carmen had an abortion performed at Today's Women's Medical Facility at 3250 S. Dixie Highway, Miami, Florida. She was six weeks into a pregnancy before deciding to terminate. The clinic provided "death pills" to end it all. Carmen used her bank card to pay for the procedure. The electronic transaction was the evidence used by the feds to lead them to her. She and her boyfriend had been indicted on a Secret Process, and the Assistant United States Attorney (AUSA) assigned to prosecute, thought it best to arrest Carmen this way outside the knowledge of the boyfriend, so as to flip her to spew her guts on all she'd done herself, and on him and the criminal organization he headed.

He was banking that the gamble would pay off, providing the government a star witness come time for trial. The primary target on the fed's hit list was a Miami native kingpin named Vershon Aikens. On the streets and throughout the underworld, he was known as "Reign Man," a goon to be feared without a doubt.

The data retrieved by the feds revealed Carmen made routine visits to the OB/GYN like clockwork every three months. They'd gained a step ahead of her. The gynecologist was contacted in advance and made aware of the situation. She related to them when Carmen's next appointment was scheduled. The elder, white female M.D. had no problem

4

contributing to setting up her black female patient. The doctor was told to keep quiet about everything.

Days later, Carmen was there in the lobby waiting to be seen. She was then called to the examination station. She'd met her judicious fate in that instance. There were four FBI officials to greet her. Two males and two females. Her mouth flung open at the sight of them. They were draped in those blue and maize colored jackets they became notorious for wearing at all arrest sites. The large bold "FBI" fonts stood out terrifyingly.

"Carmen Jenine Margaux?" asked Kate Lindsey, the female who was responsible for frisking and cuffing Carmen.

"I am."

"FBI! You're under arrest."

"Wait a minute, what! How so! I ain't committed no crime!" she let out. It was to no avail.

They began to slap the heavy metal brackets onto her wrists and read Carmen her rights.

"You have the right to remain silent. Anything you say can and will be used against you in a court of law. You have a right to an attorney. If you cannot afford one, one will be appointed to represent you. . ."

Carmen burst into tears. It was too little too late for the emotions. The feds didn't give a flying fuck one way or another. They had a job to do.

Once they'd reached the FBI Field Office at 2030 SW 145th Avenue in Miramar, Carmen was informed of the seventeen-count indictment she was being charged with. They also made her aware she faced twenty-five years to life if convicted. She was then presented with a *"proffered"* deal that essentially qualified her for immunity from prosecution on the condition she cooperated. The girl left no stone upturned in ratting. Her reason for doing so, she felt, was due to the boyfriend Reign Man, being sexually involved with her first cousin, Misty. And not only that.

The bodyguard of her kingpin boyfriend had blown out the brains of her male cousin Ralo in her presence, as he tried to resolve the dispute between the two females, while Reign Man approached them. Carmen relayed their entire relationship. All the years of their dealings. Also, she gave a detailed account of the boyfriend's drug empire. She knew a lot.

***

Months Prior . . .

Carmen and Ralo, made their way to the home Carmen shared with Reign Man. The two wanted to confront him about all he and Misty had going on. It wasn't good for the Margaux family, nor was it good for business. Not to mention, the money Ralo owed Reign Man behind a large amount of heroin being fronted him, hadn't been paid. The sight of the two together pissed the ruthless kingpin off more.

"Vershon, we need to talk to you," Carmen initiated.

She and Reign Man had a falling out not long before the day. He'd kicked her out. Carmen was staying at a hotel suite.

"And I brought Ralo with me because he wanted to talk to you as well."

"I'm sure this nigga got some shit to talk to me about. Like paying me my motherfuckin' bread he owe!" Reign Man responded. He then let them inside.

Ralo spoke up. "I'm aware I owe you, Reign. I understand all that. And I'm sure you already know I'mma pay you—"

"When, nigga! I need that!" Reign Man barked. "It's been long enough. Ain't it's about time you tighten me up already?" he spat.

"In due time. But that's not why I'm here."

"Well, why the fuck are you here, nigga!"

Ralo took Reign Man's words as an insult.

6

"I came to know, why the fuck you put your fuckin' hands on my cousin! That's why I'm here!"

Reign Man and his homie/bodyguard, Threat, took a hard look at one another. They'd felt some tension and bass in Ralo's voice. It was like he so-called himself trying to check Reign Man or something. Like he may have had a gat on him. They then gauged his energy and body language so to make a clear determination of what his intentions were. Ralo had to be strapped, with the way he'd gotten all *brolic* and shit.

Reign Man returned his attention back on Ralo. "How the fuck you gonna make it your business to come to my crib, and question me on how I treat and deal with *my* bitch! *My* baby mama! I don't give a damn if she is your cousin! Fuck boy!"

"Nigga!" Ralo came back with the same energy. He now had his hand clutched on to the pistol in his waistband he'd brought along, in the event shit was to get out of hand. He got up in Reign Man's face. They both snarled at one another. Suddenly Reign Man lashed out and smacked the shit out of Carmen.

Whop!

"You stupid bitch! How the fuck you gonna put some other nigga in my motherfuckin' business!" he spat.

Carmen was now down on the floor. If anything, Carmen should have known better.

Ralo then whipped his pistol out and cocked it. Why the fuck would he do that? He signed his own death certificate with such a move. Sometimes it's best to let sleeping vicious dogs lie where they may.

Boom!

A shot was fired.

Boom-Boom-Boom!

Threat pumped three more slugs from his Desert Eagle .50 caliber into the body of Ralo for good measure. The first was a head shot. It exploded like a tomato being hit with a baseball bat.

Ralo's ass was now dead as shit! He should have known better than to come at Reign Man like that. Of all people. And, especially so by putting himself in the middle of some "boyfriend-girlfriend" cheating on one another shit. That just can't happen. He lost his life trying to stick up for his two female cousins, when all he had to do was stay the fuck out of it and remain in his own lane. Some people never learn until it's too late.

PART ONE

"We're deep in this shit together now, whether we like it or we don't. So, we may as well go ahead and embrace the drama and the idea of it all. It's me and you, nigga! 'Beauty and the Beast!' A Kitty and a big Dog! We're in love and we're after money. Something has got to give! By any means!

-Charlotte

One

Years Prior...

Carmen came to America at a young age from Trinidad and Tobago. She was seven at the time her mother took residence in Miami. Carmen had two younger siblings as well. It didn't take long for "Miss Carmen the Beautiful" to figure out the type of power and control a female could have, if she possessed a sexy body and seductive dance moves to go along with it. She became aware of this upon coming of age. The moment she'd filled out body-wise, her feminine qualities came to life. Carmen put her exclusive dancing abilities on full display at eighteen in the top strip clubs Miami housed. She took on the stage name, "Caramel Carmen" or simply "Caramel.'"

To her credit, she'd learned the art of dancing in the native Trinidad. The country was rich in Carnival tradition. Specifically, Monday and Tuesday before Ash Wednesday. Trinidad is also a festive host of food and music to complement the dance theater.

Each summer, the family would visit and maintain close ties with relatives of the Caribbean nation. Carmen continued to do so up in age and maturity.

Carmen faced a dilemma at nineteen. Find a job to work and earn a wage or create a job and make a profit. She had three things going in her favor at the time. One, she lived in Miami, one of the sexiest cities in the country. Two, she knew how to dance really good. And three, she had a banging-ass body to cash in on. Her shape couldn't be denied. Shorty had it going on in a major way. No lie. She was of average height and kept a fit figure. The stage name matched her skin complexion. It was creamy in tone and radiant in lubrication. Her honeydew melon sized breasts were a 36-DD. They sat proper. She had low mileage sexually. But her desire and drive were in high gear. She didn't give too much of herself away to no man. The young sensation had three specialty piercings. A tongue ring, belly ring at the navel, and a mini hoop door knocker situated at the entrance of her house of love. Only certain dudes had access to this.

There was a lavish party being held at Club LIV. It was the birthday of a high-profile dope boy kingpin of the city. A dude who went by the name "Reign Man." Carmen and her bestie Shug, attended with her. Of the plethora of bad cuties who seeded the place, Carmen stood out in a higher degree. She just had this foreign type of exotic glow about herself. She had a regal presence.

As she gracefully slid about through the club in her fifteen-hundred-dollar clear lens Gucci frames and sipped on a shot of Cîroc chased with pineapple juice. She captured the attention of a special someone. In addition to her hair being on fleek and rocking a pair of diamond studded earrings to match the sparkle of her teeth as she smiled, the dude of the hour, Reign Man, looked on in awe of how this one particular chick had others spellbound. Males and females alike.

"Aye, yo, Breezy! Who the fuck is she?" Reign Man asked of his long-time friend. They'd been cool many years. He was referring to Carmen. She and Shug stood nearby in VIP.

Breezy knew exactly who he was speaking of. "Talkin' 'bout shorty in the red dress with the matching high heels?"

"You better know it! Damn, she's nice!"

"She is nice, isn't she? I believe I've seen her a time or two in the past. Probably at King of Diamonds. Or on one of those exclusive videos on a website showcasing top earner in the stripping business."

"So, she strips?" Reign Man asked.

"I wouldn't term it like that. As you can see, she does have a sense of class and taste about herself," Breezy complimented. He made sense to his friend.

"Shit! I see!" Reign Man let out.

Carmen and Shug continued to vibe and groove to the music. It was a track by Nicki Minaj.

Carmen sipped through a neon-colored straw that glowed in the day. It was as if she'd been paid millions to endorse the straw product. She was fabulous. If it wasn't known, most would think she was the birthday host herself, and not the actual person.

As for her girlfriend Shug, (short for "Sugar,") she possessed a totally different style in contrast to Carmen. Her background. Originally, she hailed from Pompano Beach, Florida. She'd grown up working in the blazing hot orange groves in the region to pay for school clothes, and to also help her big sister pay bills. Due to Shug's exposure to the South Florida sun, she was very dark in complexion. However, sultry, silky, and smooth. She prided herself on healthy eating, maintaining a slim figure, and dental hygiene. The two ladies dubbed themselves, "Mocha and Chocolate."

"What you got in mind, Reign?" Breezy asked.

"That shouldn't be too hard to figure out, lil bruh. It's two of us, and two of them. Besides, it's my birthday, my nigga. Why can't I have what I want on my special day?"

Breezy smiled at the wits of his homie.

"Like always, the right man with the right plan." Breezy stroked his ego. "And when my day arrives, we gonna do the same. Bet?"

"No doubt, nigga! All the time. That's why they call me 'Reign Man.' Because when I get better, so does everyone around me," he gloated.

He gave his right-hand man a dap, then explained the mission at once.

I need you to head over to the bar and have the head bartender to pay me a visit right quick," Reign Man instructed Breezy.

He then sat back on the lounge couch, crossed his legs, puffed on an expensive Cuban cigar, and hit a shot of the dark liquor that caused him to feel grand. It was *Paul Masson.*

Breezy weaved through the crowd to the bar. He made occasional glances at Carmen and Shug, as they popped their flavor and outshine the other female duos in the building.

Nearly five minutes later, Breezy returned to where Reign Man was located. He and Polly, the head bartender.

"What's up, Reign Man? What the hell you want?" she greeted him with a smile.

Polly always acted as if she was everybody's auntie. She also knew Reign Man's request for her would guarantee a tip of anywhere north of five hundred. He loved to tip and pay like he had weight. And man, was he heavy in the game. He and Polly were already familiar with one another from his past visits there, also from around the way. She was a Carol City girl. He was a Carol City goon.

"Polly, those two females over there near the bar," he said, pointing in the direction he was referring to.

"Those two females over there near the bar!" she retorted. "Which two?"

Reign Man gave her a look as if to say, *your ass know exactly which two I'm talking about!*

"Be for real, Polly!" he let out jokingly. He then pulled out a large roll of hundred-dollar bills.

It was obvious which two he was speaking of. They stood out in a major way for some reason. Mocha and Chocolate. Carmen had on a red dress, and Shug had on a white one.

Polly produced a pleasant smile at the sight of the "blue cheese" C-notes Reign Man was ready to lay on her. She then turned her head to have a look at who it was that had the attention of the mighty Reign Man. Carmen and Shug now stood apparent in her view.

"I believe I know which two you talking about now," Polly finally acknowledged.

Reign Man peeled five big heads from his knot, one by one. "I figured it wouldn't take too long to see what I see. Who I'm curious about."

"Which one you like? Miss Cîroc with pineapple juice? Or Miss Seagram's Gin with orange juice?" she asked. She had served their drinks.

"Polly! Take a good look at me," Reign Man muttered with humor.

She did so with a smile.

He went on, "When has a nigga who's blacker than my black ass ever desired a female that's blacker than he is? Please tell me that so I'll know."

"Ha!" Polly blurted in laughter. "Your black ass got a sense of humor, don't you, boy! You got a point though. You're right. So, it's the one with the Trinidad colored shirtdress for you, right?"

"Oh, she's from Trinidad, huh?"

"She's got those type of features and repping the colors. So, I would think so. I was watching *Love & Hip Hop: Atlanta*, and Karlie Redd and the crew took a vacation there. That's her homeland," Polly relayed.

"Oh, ok. I understand now. You're familiar with the colors in that sense. But look, you know who I want. And my nigga Breezy, is attracted to the other one. Go over and put a bug in their ear and let 'em know what the move is. That the birthday boy wants them to come over and celebrate with us, over this way. Also, a bottle of what they drinking on me. Put it in their hands with some cups. Their chase drinks too. And be sure to let her know exactly who Reign Man is too. Okay?" he carefully instructed.

"I got you, big-timer. Trust that," Polly responded and then extended her hand to retrieve the five hundred Reign Man treated her to.

"It's plenty more where that came from. You know I love to tip," he said, and stood to his feet in the four thousand-dollar Prada outfit he had on—slacks and a silk shirt, vest, bowtie, cuff links and belt. The custom-made handcrafted wing tip Italian shoes cost eight grand by themselves. He looked like money. He smelled like money. And presented himself like he was royalty. Dude was a boss nigga for real and had a grip on the game like a pitbull in a dog fight.

***

Polly immediately got on the job. First, she went to the bar to get the bottles and chasers they were drinking. From there, she approached.

"Excuse me, sweetheart. I was told to give you this," Polly said to Carmen.

"Why, thank you," Carmen replied and gladly accepted. "And who might this generous fella be who wanted us to have this?"

"Believe it or not, it's the birthday boy himself."

"Oh, wow! Really? That's sweet of him."

"Yep. And not only that."

"Oh, there's more?" asked Carmen.

"As you know, it has to be something extra to complement the genuine gesture," Polly remarked.

"Ah! You don't say," Carmen frowned, as if taken totally by surprise. "So, what's more?"

"Well, he and his friend, wants you and your friend, to come over and join them and party."

"Really!" Carmen capped in emphasis, jarring her head and shoulders, placing the free hand over her heart, her right hand.

"Yes!" Polly confirmed with a smile. "There he is," she then stated, pointing at Reign Man as he made himself visible to them.

Breezy stood next to him. Reign Man winked at her. They weren't too far away in distance.

Carmen leaned over to whisper something into Shug's ear. She then took a look towards Reign Man and Breezy. Shug smiled to confirm the acceptance of the invitation. The sultry female duo then sashayed through the crowd, en route to the direct presence of the dudes who had them on their radar.

Upon approaching, Shug stepped to Breezy and Carmen to Reign Man.

"I got your message," Carmen stated. "I'm here. So, what's poppin'!" She had no level of shyness about herself.

"I see. I like your style already," Reign Man whispered into her ear in a sensual way. The scent of peppermint from his breath permeated, invading her nostrils in the process. He smiled at her.

"I think I like your style as well, birthday boy," she responded with a bright smile of her own. "I'm Carmen. A pleasure to meet you," the beautiful bombshell introduced herself, and extended her hand to shake his.

He planted a tender kiss on the top of her hand, and then another.

"Double the delight, so you get two," he charmed her in his ways.

Carmen eyed him from head to toe, then from top to bottom, holding in position directly into those brown eyes he possessed. He went back to work with his words.

"Carmen, you say, huh? You got it going on, beautiful."

"So I've been told."

"That may be true. But with Reign Man providing such a compliment, it adds a unique quality to it."

"I'd like to hear more. I'm all ears. Maybe you can inform me more on this unique quality you speak of," Carmen responded, now looking to be amused with his seductive speech. "And I ain't got no problem doing so. You can have it however you like," he declared with a smile.

***

Reign Man and Breezy entertained the two lovely ladies well enough to go to the next level. They all exchanged numbers and carried on in VIP for the remainder of the night. Throughout, Carmen observed many impressive people (mostly dudes) approach and give praise to Reign Man. To a great degree at that. She was intrigued and now thirsty to know more about him. Even more so than he desired to know about her. He managed to reverse the game on her. It was a certain type of philosophy he knew how to put into play.

Reign Man popped shit and swallowed spit in a way like no other, palming a stack of money in one hand and had an arm around a cute bad bitch with the other. Carmen. He was *that dude*. There was no doubt about it.

17

Two

Four weeks later...

Reign Man and Carmen maintained heavy communication from the night at the club. He'd taken her out on two separate dates. She was wined and dined as if he'd courted a princess. The gentleman in him was brought out. Her wardrobe was upgraded to nothing but the best. Carmen received all the expected benefits that came along with a female of her stock being involved with a kingpin as Reign Man was. And the best part about it, he didn't try to press her in any type of way sexually. She knew from there she couldn't go wrong with him.

I'm damn sure glad I accepted his invitation to VIP that night at the club, she often thought.

She had the freedom to be herself with him, and likewise, him with her. Their friendship gained strength. He welcomed her the opportunity to stay with him. A key was given. He also put her in a car of her liking. A 5-series BMW. Dude truly liked Carmen. And it showed.

Her eagerness to get to the intimate part was expressed more so than his. His physique and the way his clothes fit, turned her on. She always found herself googly-eyed over the print of his private area. Her desire to have it came out.

The two had returned from a social event one night. They'd gotten out of the clothes they had on into something more suited to sleep in. They sat atop the bed watching the HBO hit television series, *Boardwalk Empire*. Reign Man loved that show.

Carmen eased under his arm and cuddled. "Vershon, once again, I wanna tell you thanks for all you've done in providing for me and my family." Her gratitude was expressed. "You're welcome, baby. No problem. No problem at all," he responded, real cool and nonchalant.

She then kissed him on the neck slowly and passionately, using her right hand to tenderly stroke his manhood beneath his boxer shorts. This was the first time she'd actually touched on him in this way. She never knew exactly what he was working with. Until now.

"Oh my!" she let out, clearly impressed at the size and girth of the dick.

Reign Man smiled. "What? Don't stop now. You done brought it to life." He now had a mean hard-on. "So, you might as well keep going."

Dude had a horse dick. It was a foot long. Solid like a slab of concrete.

Carmen gripped and stroked it, gearing from side to side like a stick-shift. She then disappeared under the cover to suck him off. The blanket flowed up and down as she bobbed on the dick. He was large and in charge.

Throughout the years of being sexually active, mostly as a teenager, he'd been deprived on many occasions by females being unwilling to let him penetrate. He was too large. They couldn't handle the BBC he was working with. And anytime he wanted a piece of pussy, he had to go out to the streets to get it from either prostitutes or crack-whores. They were the ones who had no walls and were deeper than an ocean. Older veteran females could handle the dick. They preferred nothing less. At times, Reign Man still managed to make soup of their insides. Especially when he pounded like a jackhammer. *Pain is love and love is pain.* It's all fair in love as it is in war.

Carmen popped her lips and tongue on the head of the dick. Reign Man tinged with tension behind the minute level of pain he felt. She nicked him a time or so with her teeth.

He was simply too large for her mouth. Nonetheless, he was used to it from times past. It was known what to expect. *Damn! This nigga got a big ass dick!* Carmen thought. *What the fuck I done got myself into? I can't back out now. Besides, I really like Vershon. And we're in too deep. I may as well get used to it.* Her thoughts ran wild.

Carmen came from under the cover. They both got completely naked. Reign Man lay back onto the bed. She grabbed a bottle of body oil from the top of the dresser, poured a handful into her palm, then glazed the dick to add lubrication. She also massaged a portion between her legs. Baby girl was now ready to take on the dick for as long as she could.

Reign Man looked on at Carmen and her sexy body. He lay back with his hands locked together behind his head and his dick standing tall. She straddled him and situated the head at the entrance of her love nest. Little by little and inch by inch, she worked the oversized pussy beater inside of her. He was now fully in her world. Dude gave her all the pleasure she could ask for. It was worth it. The wait was over. They were now all the way locked in.

Reign Man gripped Carmen tightly around the waist and held her steady as he thrust his hips and speared her in penetration drills. She was now stretched open. Her walls had been broken to his size. She panted and moaned. A wince or so came about throughout the interval. She palmed his chest, squeezing and scratching, until she found comfort as the pain faded. Then they rotated. "Mr. Big" desired to take control. He laid her on her back, parted her legs, then plunged deep into her pool. She was wet as ever.

Reign Man worked her slowly, shifted gears, and picked up the pace in modes of banging. He spit on his manhood to maintain lubrication. Dude continued to stroke and pound until the point of reaching his moment of climax. A moment he'd long awaited, since the night of the club when his flame of lust was lit behind her sex appeal. He exploded deep inside of her. His seed flooded her womb. He simply lay atop her, unloading. He'd drained completely. His juices flowed no more.

Carmen hung halfway off the bed. Her head was tilted backwards. Reign Man had his large hands locked around her throat, choking. She adored that rough shit at times and could be both naughty and nice throughout her sexual activities. She put to use the two options that night, being naughty and nice, as their sex life began from there moving forward.

Meanwhile . . .

The relationship between Breezy and Shug began to take root. They also had chemistry as a couple. People would often smile at the sight of them out in public together. Double dating with Reign Man and Carmen was always a pastime of theirs, when the guys weren't too preoccupied with handling business in the streets.

In addition to the dating thing they'd done together, Reign Man and Breezy made their girlfriends totally aware of their drug dealing lifestyle. As if they didn't already know. However, by them being open and straight up about everything, they gained the respect of the girls. They wanted to get down and make moves with their men, so as to be of aid and assistance in the hustle and make their own paper in the process. Nothing makes a dope boy's dick harder and more motivated to be a better version of himself than his girl wanting to risk it all with him and do everything he needed her to do. Without telling him no. And without being a problem or a headache.

Reign Man had always properly supplied Breezy with product throughout the years. He made sure his homie had the material necessary to earn a decent living and make good of himself. There wasn't a need to have him tagging along, if he wasn't trying to get rich and elevate in the game to a higher level. Breezy was himself a million-dollar dude in the dope game and had legitimate businesses to clean up the dirty money. He and Reign Man both had Shug and Carmen transporting for them and doing deals. Everyone was all in at this point. The family members of the girls and all. They had business together.

***

Carmen eventually ended up pregnant. They were both excited at the fact that their first child was soon to be brought into the world. To make her feel more comfortable, Reign Man bought a mansion for them in Coral Gables. It was an estate situated in an affluent gated community. The cost was two-point-two million.

Reign Man's sister, Cheyenne, took a liking to Carmen, and the two clicked at the onset. They'd spent a lot of time together getting familiar with one another. The girls loved to shop and spend the kingpin's money. However, Carmen was a homebody in a lot of ways and placed great emphasis on preparing the place for their daughter to arrive. Home is where she was the majority of the time when not at her mother's or with her siblings or Shug.

The closer the day approached for Carmen to give birth, the more Reign Man did all he could to keep her situated and there in place at home, all the way out the way. From police, haters, enemies, and any unfortunate scenarios that could harm her any type of way, including car accidents, spiteful females, circulating germs in society, etc.

Shug and Cheyenne were too busy living their lives and handling business with their men. Reign Man supplied Cheyenne's boyfriend as well, so Cheyenne couldn't spend as much time with Carmen as they once did. And her sisters were off in college gaining a higher learning. Therefore, to have company and beat boredom, Carmen persuaded one of her female cousins to leave Trinidad and Tobago to come to America to live. That way, they could be close and enjoy one another again as they had in their youth.

Her name was Misty, Carmen's favorite female cousin. They looked alike, had the same type of figure, and thought in similar ways. Only, Misty was younger. And had a side to her now that Carmen wasn't aware of. She made the journey to the States to take residence.

Carmen's dependency on Reign Man blinded her to many things. She was able to overlook much of it. However, certain occurrences simply were too obvious to ignore.

When Misty first arrived, she didn't have much money and dressed nowhere near as expensive as she now did. She had a new Lexus, owned a hair salon, and lived in a posh apartment loft in Boca Raton of all places, an area where only people with money lived. In the four months she'd been there in Miami, Misty had really come up. But for a single woman with no kids, that shouldn't have been a difficult feature to accomplish. Fortunately for Carmen, she was able to see through the bullshit and managed to put two and two together.

Reign Man had gotten careless in how he went about his dealings with Misty. Truth be, he really didn't give a fuck. He was Reign Man. Who could tell him otherwise?

He utilized the apartment he'd situated Misty in as a stash house for money and drugs. Carmen had no knowledge of exactly where her cousin lived. She'd begun to pick up on things at the point of Misty coming around more to deliver Reign Man large amounts of money as time progressed. She made runs out of town for dude. In the beginning of this, Carmen originally thought Misty had a boyfriend who moved the product, and wanted to keep a secret on who supplied her. She was lost on what was really going on. Even though it was right under her nose.

Shug was pregnant herself around this time. She and Carmen adored the idea. She paid her friend a visit one day.

It had been just over a month since they'd last seen one another physically. The two had so much to discuss.

"So, what's been good with you? Everything smooth between you and Breezy?" Carmen initiated.

They were in the den area of the house. Reign Man, Breezy, and their homie Threat, were all out back in the pool house having a conversation themselves.

"Yeah, everything been good between us. I'm glad to have that man in my life. Breezy Keye is a good dude, you hear me," Shug replied. "What about you and Reign Man? Y'all good? Reason I ask, I know you, boo-boo. Something not right. What is it?" she then asked.

Carmen looked at her friend and shook her head in a disgusted way.

"Shug, I got good reason to believe Vershon got other things going on with other females behind my back. And that's not right. I'm pregnant with our daughter. And I stay cooped up in this damn house all day, not able to get out and about. But shit cool though. He can continue to frolic and have all the fun he so pleases. So long as I'm taken care of and got shit in my own name to fall back on," Carmen declared.

"I still believe it's more to it than you're telling me, Carmen. And the way you sound, I believe it's really personal," Shug stated to compel her friend to give her the real story.

Carmen produced a concerned look. "Come closer, girl. You gotta hear this." A tear streamed down her face.

Shug got up from her seat and stepped over to where Carmen sat. "So, what's up, girl? Talk to me. You already know that no matter what, I'm right here with you. Right?"

"I know, girl, I know. But this shit too fucking much!"

"What is it, Carm? Talk to me, please."

Carmen exhaled and dropped her head low, shaking from side to side again. "How 'bout I found out, Vershon so-called himself fuckin' my cousin Misty," she revealed.

"Get the fuck outta here, Carmen!" Shug exclaimed. She couldn't believe her ears. "And how exactly did you find out about this? I'm dying to know," Shug asked and didn't beat around the bush about it.

"I messed around and came across receipts to a suite he had in Las Vegas at the Bellagio Hotel and Resort. Room two twenty-two."

"Stop playing, Carm!"

"No shit, girl. I'm dead ass. When you ever known me to bullshit like this?"

"Never! That's how I know you for real. But how does Misty play a part in all this?"

"Because, her dumb-ass had the fucking nerve to go live on *Instagram* and post pictures and shit, bragging about being at a five-star hotel and casino called the Bellagio! In room two twenty-two!"

"But how you figure she had to be there with Reign Man?" Shug asked a legit question.

"Because . . . that was just too much of a coincidence for it to have not been him. In one of the videos the bitch posted, I caught a glimpse of those red bottom sneakers I bought Vershon. I also noticed his favorite watch. That expensive *Patek*. It was on the nightstand. And on top of that, the bitch went so far as to mention the fact, she was laid up with a boss in Sin City. A play-maker out the Port of Miami, with the initials R.M. Now how much more did I need to see and hear before coming to the conclusion it was Vershon 'Reign Man' Aikens she was talking about? I seen his shoes. And I seen his feet. He was away that weekend. Supposedly on business! At least that's the lie he told me. And I found the receipt to the hotel Misty bragged about. My cousin, that is. That's clear enough for you?" Carmen stated.

"Well, damn! That's a lot to digest. But you seem to be right. You bring it to their attention?"

"Nope. Not yet. I'm trying to wait until the right time to do so. If I decide to at all. I'm pregnant and shit, Shug. I don't need no negative energy in my life right now. And I also know she's going to say something or do something to expose the shit they got going on more. That's a dumb bitch!" Carmen spat.

Shug shook her head from side to side. She felt bad at the predicament her dear friend found herself in. Her own flesh and blood first cousin turned out to be a snake.

"Family ain't shit sometimes! Blood not thicker than water all the time. And a nigga may not be as loyal and true as he makes himself out to be. No matter how deep in the game he may be, or how much respect in the streets he may have, all niggas got the potential to fall weak and get sloppy with how they shaking and moving," Shug declared.

She was able to paint a clear picture for Carmen with words and make the reality of Reign Man an ugly sight right before her eyes.

Three

Months Later . . .

Carmen gave birth to a baby girl. She weighed eight pounds, four ounces. She and Reign Man named their beautiful daughter Ni'Asia Chernell Aikens. Reign Man wasted no time spoiling their firstborn. He bought some of everything for the little one. Things she wasn't even big enough to enjoy yet.

And on the flip side, he didn't waste any time having Carmen get back to business and hitting the road, transporting kilos of his product. She was set to take a trip up the Florida Turnpike to Tampa. Reign Man previously lived there. He had family who resided there, also customers. In particular, he had a cousin. A cat by the name of Travis Miller, aka "T-Man." He'd not long gotten free from state prison and was back in the dope game, looking to come up again. This was to be Carmen's first time meeting him. They'd never done so before. And it was her second trip to Tampa for Reign Man.

"Look baby," Reign Man initiated. "Here's one of my burner phones. When you get close to Tampa, I need you to hit my people T-Man up and let him know you almost there. He should be ready for you. He's gonna have a rental car ready for you too. You already know what to do from there. Switch cars, get the money, check into a motel to get a little sleep, and then come on back home with the money."

Reign Man gave clear instructions to her on exactly what to do. He was holding their daughter and standing in the doorway of the car Carmen sat in as they talked. The vehicle was loaded with dope hidden in secret compartments.

Carmen looked on at his face sternly from behind her dark Prada shades. The blackened lenses were meant to hide her hurt and pain. The fact that her dude secretly carried on a sexual affair with her cousin ripped her apart internally.

"I understand. I got you. But I was wondering, does Tampa got a Bellagio Hotel and Casino too that I can check into for the night to rest up?" Carmen sarcastically stated.

She'd been holding back for months. Not anymore.

"What?" Reign Man muttered. He looked at her with a damning expression. Carmen's words were heard clearly. No mistaking that.

He found himself brainstorming there in the moment, seeking to figure out how Carmen came to know.

"What you say, Carmen?"

"Nothing, Vershon. I didn't say anything."

He continued to look at her coldly.

"Go ahead and take care of this for me, okay? And remember, don't call anybody or any of our main phone numbers we use. You never know who might be listening in," Reign Man said.

Carmen kept quiet and said nothing more. She only looked at him.

"I'll see you when you get back," he lastly said.

She didn't respond. Only closed the door of the car, started it, and drove away.

While walking to the front door of the house, he pulled out his cellphone to call Misty. He was still holding his daughter while contacting his side piece.

"Hey, daddy! What's good?" she answered.

"Bitch, don't 'hey daddy' me! What the fuck wrong with you?" he barked.

"What, Reign Man! Why you talking to me like this!"

"Don't be acting like you ain't say shit!"

"Say shit about what!"

"How the hell Carmen know about us!"

His outburst startled his daughter. She began to cry. He attempted to calm her down.

Misty spoke on. "I don't know. I ain't say shit! I promise."

"Bye, bitch!" he insulted, then ended the call.

Two seconds later, she called back. He ignored. She called again. Same thing. And a third time. He finally answered.

"What!"

"Reign Man, look. I swear to God, bro, I ain't say shit to her or nobody else. That's on everything. You gotta believe me."

"Why should I believe you? As much as your ass like to show out and take shots at other females. I don't know how Carmen wouldn't easily find out."

"Well, it ain't come from me. Why would I fuck myself up like that?"

"You tell me!"

"That'll be crazy on my behalf, won't it?"

"It damn sho' would."

"You still ain't said what happened between you two." Misty dug deep.

"It ain't shit to concern yourself with. I got it. Everything cool. As long as you ain't did no stupid shit like post something on social media during our trip to Vegas," he warned.

It was too late. Carmen had already downloaded the video and saved the photos Misty made public.

"Can I see you?" she asked.

"What the fuck you want with me? I got too much shit to do today and to focus on, than to be bullshittin' around with you," Reign Man stated.

"Please! I need to see you. We got to make this right, sweetie."

"I'm busy, lil mama, and I ain't in the mood for all the extra shit you like to throw my way."

"Please, Vershon. I can't go on like this. Especially not with you thinking I fucked up and exposed us to Carmen," she pleaded. "Pretty please."

"You gonna give me some head when you get here? You gonna suck on this dick for me?" He loved to talk nasty to her, and she loved to hear it.

"Now, you know . . . I ain't got no problem sucking on that big motherfucka' for you! Actually, I love to," Misty responded.

She made Reign Man smile and caused him to get aroused behind her words, at the thought of the pleasure she provided him. With her wide lips, big mouth, and deep throat she had. This was the quality about her that gave her the advantage over Carmen with him. The pleasure she took in providing him oral sex. And the passion she put into her craft. Misty had good pussy too.

"Look, your ass got ten minutes to get here. Or I'mma change my mind."

"You ain't gotta tell me twice. I'm on the way now," Misty responded. She was eager to answer the call to Reign Man's wild side.

She raced to her Lexus, got in, and began the drive towards Reign Man's location. She managed to keep him on the phone the whole time. Misty had learned really well how to keep his attention.

***

Hours later that day . . .

The night was setting in. The dark sky now covered the Sunshine State. Carmen reached the outskirts of the city of Tampa. She pulled out the phone Reign Man gave her. There were only contacts to customers in it. Nothing more.

That no good cheating bastard got the nerve to have me on the road taking chances for him with his drugs, while he fucking my own cousin behind my back. But it's cool. I'll have the last laugh, Carmen thought.

The tears flowed heavily. She was hurt in a major way. Her thoughts continued.

He said to call "B-Man" when near and let him know I'm almost to Tampa. And for him to have the other car ready.

Carmen was completely unsure of Reign Man's exact words. She'd paid him no attention at the time he gave her instructions on what to do. All she found herself thinking about in that moment was that receipt from the Bellagio, and the level of betrayal her cousin and boyfriend perpetrated against her.

She then pulled out her personal phone and went to the contact to call Reign Man. She had a photo of him there as the profile picture. One of him smiling, in a sinister way to her at this point. She gazed at the image angrily. A rush of madness and pain was triggered and shot throughout her body. In a tantrum, she threw the phone to the floor and banged the bottom of her fist on the dashboard.

"Motherfucka'! I hate you! I hate the both of you!" she yelled out.

She had a cool off period. Her anger went away. Not all of it though.

Fuck them! She thought once more. *I'mma be the one to come out on top. On God, I am!*

Through it all, she never gained the clarity she was supposed to on exactly who she was supposed to see, and what she was supposed to do. Besides, the car she drove was loaded with fifteen bricks of meth inside. And she didn't know who it was to go to.

Scrolling through the phone, the name "B-Man" appeared first in the order. Then there was "Keenan," "Man-Man," "Shannon," "Trouble Man," and so on and so forth. Her thoughts ran rampant. She could not recall who Reign Man said to get in touch with.

31

Fuck it! I'mma just call the first name that come up. I think this the one anyway.

It was B-Man.

"His phone rang. "Yo, what's poppin'!" he answered.

"Hey. I'm almost there," Carmen responded.

"Huh?" B-Man let out from confusion.

"It's Reign Man's girl. I'm about forty-five minutes out from Tampa. You got the rental car ready for me?"

B-Man didn't have the slightest idea on what she was talking about. However, he sensed an opportunity. As he knew how Reign Man conducted business when having his drivers transport from Miami. The two had done business the same in the past. And B-Man knew exactly where the product was hidden in the car. Underneath the back seat. A compartment panel concealed the addictive narcotics.

"Oh, you about forty-five minutes out, you say? How many dancers you brought with you?" B-Man spoke in code.

"I've got fifteen with me. They got the energy to dance all night too," Carmen comprehended and responded.

Reign Man had mentioned to her the night before how many kilos he needed her to traffic.

"Oh, you got fifteen of 'em with you, huh? And I need to have the other car ready? Where we supposed to meet?"

"At the hotel. The Hyatt Inn. I'mma be staying there." This was her usual routine on trips to Tampa. "You familiar with his way of doing things, right?"

"You got to know that. I'll be there all right?"

"All right. Talk later."

The call ended.

In addition to forgetting who she was supposed to have called, Carmen forgot about having to pick up money once the car switch was to be made. She was used to simply exchanging cars and nothing more. Reign Man would normally have the money in advance.

B-Man began to put his scheme together right then and there. He was a Blood gang member. His set claimed was

"Sex-Money-Murder," followers of the Pistol Peter Pollock's crew, and he had a whole block full of niggaz to back him up if shit was to backfire behind taking Reign Man's cookies.

B-Man needed to double check something. He wanted to be sure he had the leverage to do Reign Man dirty and get away with it long enough to arm himself. He called Carmen back at the number.

"Hello!" she answered.

"Hey. Me again. I'mma be a little behind on getting to the hotel. I gotta be sure to get you a decent ride."

"Okay. It's cool. I'mma stay the night over anyway, to rest up," Carmen replied.

"Okay. That's a bet. Also, I already know how your dude like to operate. He don't want nobody to call him while everything in motion, does he?"

"No, he doesn't. He hate it when anybody get in touch with him while the process is going. But you don't have to worry about that though. I don't want to talk to his ass or hear from him either until I get back home no way. His ass has done too much!" Her sarcasm seethed venom. It was clear there was trouble in paradise down in Miami.

B-Man caught on. He read between the lines on all she related. He then instigated.

"Ah, hell! What bitch you done caught Reign Man with now?"

"Huh!" Carmen exhaled. "I don't even wanna think about it no more. But I'll be there at the Hyatt in due time. Besides, I'm sure you already know how your cousin likes to get down with the many females he like to play around with."

My cousin! This bitch think I'm somebody else, B-Man thought.

"Yeah, cuz can be a wild boy when it comes to the females."

"His ass went too far this time! Too goddamn far!" She continued to run her mouth to someone she didn't even know.

"Y'all two should be all right though. Just chill. It'll work itself out. I promise you, it will."

"It may or may not. Who's to say."

The call ended for a second time shortly after.

B-Man returned to his thoughts. *Fuck that Miami-ass nigga! His bitch the one fucking up and delivering to the wrong person. His loss, my gain. My pleasure, his pain.*

The plan was to now go out and pay a crackhead enough money to borrow their car. It had to be a decent one. He would then exchange that particular vehicle with Carmen and drive away with the one she drove, with the work and all. The car Carmen drove was a Lexus ES. That was Reign Man's primary transport mobile. He'd bought it around the same time he bought the one for Misty.

The worst-case scenario for B-Man regarding an issue with the car he would borrow from one of his crack smoking customers, was that they could easily call the cops and report the vehicle stolen. He had a way from under that. And the greedy nature he possessed, forced him to swindle his connection out of supply, could potentially come back to haunt him in the end. He had to play it smoothly. Or else, the consequences may be severe.

B-Man's plot worked out to near perfection.

Four

One Day Later . . .

Carmen made it back to Miami. The time was just past 10:00 a.m. Reign Man was in the master bedroom watching TV. He loved to tune in to the sports program, *First Take* with the hosts Stephen A. Smith and Molly Q on *ESPN*. She exited the car and entered the front door to the mansion.

"Carmen! That's you?" Reign Man called out for her.

She was halfway up the stairs.

"Yeah! It's me," she responded. She then walked into the room.

"Reign Man now had a confused look about his face. "Why you empty-handed?" he asked.

"Huh?" She jarred her head and responded, "Oh, I left my purse downstairs."

"My people had all the money on hand? Where is it? I want to count it."

"Where is what, Vershon? What money?"

"The money for the work you transported, Carm. My cousin was supposed to have given you the money for everything."

"He was supposed to give me some money for everything?" she retorted.

Reign Man construed his face angrily. He gave her a look of outrage.

"Hell yeah, he was supposed to have given you some money for me! You didn't get anything from him?"

"No!" She stood in the middle of the floor with her hands situated on her hips.

"Carmen!"

"Vershon!" she retorted sarcastically.

"Look, how was it so hard to understand? Go to Tampa. Call my cousin 'T-Man Miller' in the phone list. Let him know when you got close to Tampa. Be ready to swap cars. Get the money he had for me. Check into the hotel to get a little rest. Then, get your ass back home with my money. What was hard about that to do?" he asked with a serious tone of voice.

"Vershon. First of all, you didn't say call 'T-Man Miller' at no time! You told me to call B-Man. And second—"

He cut her words short.

"I know goddamn well you ain't fucked up my shit, Carmen! I just know damn well you ain't!" he spat. "Where the fuck is that phone I gave you to use?"

"It's in my bag downstairs."

"Well, I suggest your stupid ass go down there to get it then!" he insulted.

"Don't call me stupid, Vershon!" she ranted then began to walk back down the stairs.

"I'll call you whatever the fuck I wanna call you! Especially when you done fucked up! Dumb ass bitch!"

Carmen was very pissed off now behind Reign Man disrespecting her with his words. He'd only called her out of her name once, before that day.

She returned to the room with her handbag and pulled the phone out. Reign Man snatched it from her.

"Don't be snatching nothing from me!" she said to him.

"I'mma do more than snatch something from your ass if you done fucked up and gave my car and my product to the wrong person! You just be patient. It's about to happen," he warned, while making a call on the phone. "How dumb can your ass really be?"

"Vershon, stop talking like that!"

36

He paid her no mind.

T-Man Miller was now on the phone. "Yeah! What it do, cuz? I thought your girl was on the way?" he questioned. He knew it was Reign Man by the number on the screen of the phone. Reign Man had sent a quick text before the call to let him know he was about to call.

"Yo, T-Man, my girl already been up that way."

"I ain't meet nobody! And I didn't get no work either!" T-Man made him aware.

"You see what the fuck your stupid ass done did!" he yelled at Carmen more. She was standing not too far away looking at him. There was nothing she could say to rectify her fuck-up.

Reign Man got back to speaking with T-Man. "Yo cuz, this slow heifer more than likely done gave my motherfuckin' car and dope to the wrong person!"

He had T-Man on speaker phone.

"I know damn well your girl ain't did no shit like that, fam! As much as you pride yourself on preparation."

Little did T-Man know, he was pouring gas on a fire that was already lit.

"More than likely, that's what has happened, cuz. I'mma hit you back in a minute, T. A'ight?"

"Bet."

The call concluded.

Reign Man turned his focus back to Carmen. He had a look about his face that clearly let her know she'd fucked up. And bad.

"You see what the fuck you done did! Not only have you cost me one of my cars, I lost over a hundred-thousand-dollars' worth of dope as well!" he spat. "Now, who the fuck did you call and make a mistake and give my shit to?"

Reign Man was now really enraged.

"I told you, Vershon. Your words to me was to call B-Man once I was almost to Tampa. And that's what I did."

"No, the fuck I didn't! I know I clearly said my cousin, T-Man. T-Man Miller. I know those were my exact words."

"Well . . . that was the person I called and met. He was who I swapped cars with. B-Man in the phone."

Reign Man and B-Man had dealt before. But that was a time long past. They had no business arrangement around the time.

At that instance, Reign Man attempted to contact B-Man, although knowing he'd been robbed by deception, and had a very low chance now of getting dude to answer. He still had the phone speaker on.

"We're sorry. You have reached a number that has been changed or no longer in service . . ."

He ended the call before the operator recording could finish. Reign Man then tried once more simply off impulse. Same results. He hated the thought of someone taking something from him. Dude began to fume with rage now. Carmen was in deep trouble.

"Carmen, how the fuck could you be so goddamn stupid!"

She put out both hands in the position to indicate *stop.* "Vershon! Please stop talking to me like that! Okay?" she yelled back. "I made a mistake. We'll get over it."

"Look, why the fuck you didn't call me if you was unsure about something!"

"Because, I didn't want to hear nothing you had to say at the time! That's why!" she fired back.

"You not wanting to hear nothing I had to say, just cost me a car and a lot of money!"

"Well . . . I made a mistake," she responded, then rolled her eyes and snaked her neck. "Ain't nothing we can do about it now."

"Oh yes, the fuck it is something we can do about it! Your dumb ass about to get busy trying to track down my shit!" he let out angrily.

"Well, if you would've been more busy taking care of business and not have your ass all out in Vegas, disrespecting me by fucking my cousin Misty, maybe this wouldn't have happened!" she said while up in his face, now on her tiptoes. She had her arms tightened and fists balled.

There was no way to take back what she'd just revealed out of anger. She may have fucked up.

"What the fuck you just say to me?" He was now about to snap.

Carmen sensed his rage on the verge of erupting. She turned and took off to run out the house and get away from him. Reign Man gave chase after her. It wasn't good for her in that moment. The heels she had on, caused her to twist her ankle and hit the floor in pain. He grabbed her by the expensive sewn-in weave she had, wrapped it around his wrist to hold her steady, then went to work on her ass. Dude spazzed.

Whop-Whop-Whop-Whop-Whop . . . Whop!

"You dumb-ass bitch! You worrying about the wrong shit, done caused you to fuck up and lose my car and my work!" he spat.

He yanked her around like a rag doll, then dragged the poor girl across the floor, leading to the stairway.

Whop!

He was able to get a clean blow in for good measure. She was caught off guard.

"Vershon! Please! I was wrong, okay?" she pleaded.

Their daughter was now awakened behind the ruckus and crying.

"Bitch, don't be trying to apologize now! You wasn't, not too long ago! Maybe none of this would be happening had you admitted you fucked up to begin with, and not be concerned about who else I got something going on with! As long as you good, that should be all that matter!"

Whop!

He smacked her again.

Wham!

Then kicked her.

"Bitch!" he continued to insult.

Reign Man then dragged her down the stairs, causing her to bang her head along the way. He had her by the ankles. His size and strength were too much for her.

The intent was to make her think over how bad she'd fucked up with the beating, then put her out the house temporarily behind her mouth.

"Now get your dumb ass on out my house!" he spat once at the bottom of the stairs. He then opened the door. "And go do something with that fuckin' car there!" he pointed. "Because I'm sure that motherfucka' hot as a firecracker right now! That ain't no rental my people went out and got!"

Whop!

He smacked her again while she was still on the floor. Reign Man then dragged her out onto the front steps and went back inside to get her purse. He temporarily locked the door.

Carmen sat and sobbed in tears like there was no tomorrow.

Reign Man returned. He opened the door. "Here, bitch!" He threw the purse at her. "Now take your ass back up that road to Tampa and find my shit!"

"Vershon. Please. My baby. What about our daughter?" she let out in a weakened voice. She'd been defeated.

"Bitch, don't worry about Ni'Asia! We good! Just go get my car and dope back! That's all you need to be doing!"

He then slammed the door and locked it, situating the sturdy latch rods from the top, sides, and bottom portions to reinforce security on the door to keep her from coming back inside.

Reign Man then called T-Man on his main phone and told him all about Carmen's fuck-up. The ass whipping as well. They had a discussion on how to best deal with the problem the nigga B-Man had now created behind the stunt he pulled.

Carmen called Shug once she took a seat in the car. She let her know she was on the way to her place, and about the fight with Reign Man. The whole story would be related once there.

Five

A Few Days Later . . .

Reign Man still found himself pissed. He wouldn't allow Carmen back into the house at the speed she thought he would. Reign Man had Cheyenne look after Ni'Asia for the time being, until he and Carmen aired out what they had going on.

Shug made her dude Breezy aware of the situation with his best friend and her best friend. She had him make an attempt to talk with Reign Man and see if he was willing to give Carmen a pass. Dude wasn't trying to hear nothing. That Lexus and the hundred-thousand lost, had him pissed. Truth be told, Breezy did the expected and sided with Reign Man. He told him he didn't blame him not one bit. That he would've done the same thing had Shug fucked up in that way.

Carmen felt violated physically. So much so, to the point of bringing the dispute to the attention of one of her male cousins who'd not long ago moved back to Miami. A dude named Chad Thompson, aka "Ralo."

Ralo was an aggressive personality himself and about that type of action. He wanted smoke now. And wanted a fade with Reign Man. Little did Carmen know, her cousin owed Reign Man twenty thousand for product he'd been fronted by dude. Ralo didn't give a fuck about any of that at that point. He didn't play behind any dude putting their paws on a female family member of his.

The plan was for Ralo and Carmen to make it their business to go and confront Reign Man and hopefully, have him see the error of his ways with what he'd done. This move was designed to put Carmen back in good standing with the boyfriend. If shit was to go awry, then Ralo felt capable to get right on that level with dude, the moment he took it there. The intent, however, was to go about it the right way.

Carmen called Reign Man and wanted to know a time and day they could talk in person and attempt to reconcile the differences they experienced. He let her know they could do so that day, six days from the moment he beat her ass. She badly wanted to return home, as she'd been at a hotel between the time.

Before she and Ralo were to show up on a surprise visit, they had another stop to make, to Misty's place. Ralo knew where she lived. He'd been by a time or two. They pulled up on their cutthroat cousin to check her about the situation. She'd dropped kitty litter on the reputation of the Margaux family, with the shit caused by fucking with her cousin's man. Misty didn't give a fuck though. Reign Man was too good to give up at that point.

Once there, Misty let them in.

"So Misty," Ralo initiated. "Look, and you better not lie to me. Because you know how your ass do."

Carmen looked on at Misty and shook her head from side to side in disgust.

"Carmen already told me her side of the story. Now, I gotta hear yours," Ralo further said.

Misty grinned mischievously at Carmen.

Before the two had arrived, Ralo gave Carmen strict orders not to say anything or react to any of the shenanigans he knew Misty would potentially put into the mix. Hence, the slick shot she took with the grin.

"What's good, Ralo? What's up!" Misty responded.

"I'mma just ask you straight up. Because you know we better than this as a family. What the fuck you and your sneaky ass got going on with Reign Man behind Carmen's back?" he asked bluntly.

Misty's mouth dropped to the floor. There was a long pause. She finally spoke out. "What you mean, 'what me and my sneaky ass got going on with Reign Man behind Carmen's back?'" she retorted. Not knowing Carmen saved the videos, the pictures, and the receipt from the Bellagio before she could delete them from her social media platforms.

Carmen's intention was to bring to Misty's attention everything she had on hand.

Ralo responded to the aggressive way Misty so-called herself talking to him. "Just what the fuck I said, is what I mean, Misty! I saw the videos and the pictures you got posted. Carmen saved them before you deleted everything," he said and made her aware.

"Ralo, I post videos and pictures all the time. What's wrong with that?" Misty let out while going back and forth between Carmen and Ralo with her eyes.

Carmen wasn't able to hold back any longer. She unleashed. "Bitch, I found a receipt from the Bellagio in Vershon's pants pockets! The same hotel you bragged about and had the nerve to record a video of his watch, his feet, and other shit I know belong to him! Do stop lying."

Ralo now had the material in his phone. He unlocked it and showed Misty the evidence. "Ain't no way you can deny anything. And just so you know, you done caused all kinds of problems in Carmen's household between her and dude. You wrong, Misty."

Misty got quiet and didn't say anything else in the moment. She thought over what Reign Man had said to her, to *"Not say anything, no matter what."* She continued to pretend to be at a loss for words.

"What's the matter, sneak bitch! Cat got your tongue? Huh!" Carmen spat.

"You better watch your fucking mouth, Carmen! Real shit, hoe! You in my place!" Misty fired a shot back.

"Bitch! You the hoe! You the one can't get a man on your own and got to go out to be with another woman's man! Not me!"

"Well bitch, if you was doing what the fuck you was supposed to and taking care of your man, he wouldn't be so busy trying to be all up in my ass!"

Carmen snapped. "Bitch!" she spat, then lunged at Misty. Ralo had to get between them.

He wrapped Carmen up and tossed her over his shoulder. He then exited the apartment and headed to the car. Misty locked the door behind them. She looked on as they drove away.

At that point, Misty grabbed her phone to call Reign Man to let him know what had happened.

"Yeah. What up, lil momma," he answered.

"Hey, I don't know how, but Carmen knows about us. Her and Ralo so-called themselves stopping by here to check me about the shit," she informed.

"Oh yeah?" he responded without a care in the world.

"Hell yeah. And they on the way to you now to do the same. I called to let you know. I guess they aim to check you too."

"I'm Reign Man, Misty. I do all the checking on my end. Never forget that."

"Well, they on the way."

"A'ight. Thanks for the heads up," he lastly said, then ended the call.

He took a look over towards his homie who was there with him. It was Threat. He'd heard what Misty related. The two had a light laugh at the thought of Ralo putting himself in the mix. They were in the den area of the house, plotting on how to get back at B-Man for taking his shit. Things went from one issue to the next. From bad to ugly just like that.

Had Ralo known any better, he would've gone about things in a different way. However, he didn't.

***

Carmen looked on in total shock at Ralo down on the floor. There was a strip of brain tissue hanging from his head caused by the gunshot wound. He also had three holes in the center of his chest, like those in a bowling ball.

"Vershon! What the fuck!" she yelled out. "What the fuck just happened!" Her words had a grave tone to them.

She looked back and forth from Reign Man to Threat, to Reign Man again. It was as if she was going through stages of delusional compulsion. The dream-like effect.

"Damn, Threat!" Reign Man let out. He was struggling to gain his hearing following the gunshots.

"What else was I supposed to do! The nigga drew down on you, Reign!" Threat responded. "He threatened your life."

Threat then took a look down at Carmen. When the first shot was fired, she was already plopped low. Threat had a questioning demeanor. The bodyguard was ready to whack her as well. He had to wait and see what Reign Man's decision would be.

Reign Man locked eyes with him. There was a long pause as he heavily contemplated what to do with his girlfriend, who could now potentially be an eyewitness to murder. He spoke out.

"Carmen. What happened here just then is not to ever be spoken of, okay? Ever!" he ordered with a serious meaning to his tone. "Do I make myself clear, Carmen?"

"Yes, Vershon. We're clear on that. I haven't seen anything. And I don't know anything," Carmen responded in compliance.

"And when your cousin Ralo dropped you off at home, after you two left the apartment of the other cousin, Misty, you don't know what happened to Ralo, and hadn't seen him anymore from that point, right?"

He coached her on exactly what to say.

"Right," she replied, then went silent and said no more.

Reign Man looked at Threat and shook his head, indicating "no." He wanted him to put his gun away. Threat had it trained on Carmen. His trigger finger itched. He was ready to scratch the scalp between the hair trigger of the weapon.

"You making a big mistake, Reign. I'm telling you, bro. Let me do her!" Threat requested once more. He seriously wanted to kill Carmen.

"Threat! I said no, bro! It's cool. We're good," Reign Man denied him again.

Threat then reluctantly put his gun away. It still had a warmth to it from the four rounds he'd put down Ralo with.

Reign Man then took a squat low over Carmen to speak to her. "Carm, look. This what I want you to do, okay? I want you to get up, go to the room, and pack as much needed for you and Ni'Asia, and prepare to leave. I'm sure you got enough money on your bank card. But in the event you don't, I'mma send you more through *Zelle* and *Chime*. I want you to go on a month-long vacation to Trinidad to visit your people. I know your mom wanna see y'all. She hasn't had a chance to since she moved back. I'll be down there myself in a week or so. I've got some business to take care of while I'm down there, too," Reign Man said.

"Okay, Vershon. That's fine. I understand," she replied to his direct order.

He let her get to her feet and watched her walk towards the bedroom to pack up.

The clean-up process and the disposal of Ralo's half-headed body began then and there.

"Threat, call the clean-up man and y'all get this together for me, a'ight, bro?" Reign Man stated to the bodyguard friend.

"I'm on it, bro. But I'm telling you, that's gonna come back to haunt us in the long run," Threat declared, stabbing his finger through the air in the direction where Carmen went.

Reign Man walked out the house headed toward the pool area out back. He needed some fresh air.

Threat pulled out his phone to call a guy Reign Man had on payroll for bloody, messy situations. The remaining portion of Ralo's head was a nasty mess too. Brain spatter, globs of thick blood, and skull fragments littered the place. They had a serious clean-up job on their hands.

Six

Three Weeks Later...

The troubled couple, Reign Man and Carmen, were now down in her native Trinidad and Tobago. They found themselves walking along the beach, having a much-needed conversation. Reign Man arrived in the country the day before. Carmen wanted to clearly let him know how she felt about everything that had occurred between them.

"Vershon, I'm very traumatized behind that incident with Ralo," she stated.

"Carmen, now I know we went over this already. We ain't got no business continuing to talk about it," he responded.

"I have to let you know. Because I can't sleep. I barely eat. I suffer from PTSD behind it. And I'm bad off because of it."

"You saw exactly what Ralo did to bring that on himself. He pulled a gun on me. My life was put in danger first, you know. My bodyguard did what he was supposed to have done. Protect me," Reign Man stated and paused to have a look at her. He anticipated her comeback. "By the way, why the fuck you bring that nigga to my house anyway?" Reign Man asked a legit question he hadn't before.

The two stopped walking. Carmen looked him sternly into the eyes. She went on to speak her piece.

"Vershon, I know everything about you and my cousin Misty. The sleazy bitch admitted it to me and Ralo."

Reign Man jarred his head and began to bite at the lining on the inside of his jaws. The revelations startled him in a way. He had to think of something to counter with.

"Say what?"

She repeated herself for him. "I said, I know everything about you and my cousin Misty. That the sleazy bitch admitted it to me and Ralo."

There was no longer any level of fear on her part. She was ready to fully address the elephant in the room.

"Carm, listen to yourself."

"No, Vershon! You listen to me!" she snapped back defiantly. "I know you took that girl on a trip to Las Vegas with you. I got all the facts to prove it."

He offered nothing to defend himself. Only looked on at her and shook his head in defeat.

"And I just told you the no-good bitch actually admitted it. I saved her videos and photos."

Carmen then tapped the button on her phone to play the recordings. Reign Man heard Misty for himself.

"Not only that, Vershon. Have a look at these."

She went to the gallery in the phone to present more of the evidence.

"Anything look familiar to you?" she asked, referring to the things that belonged to him. She then pulled the hotel receipt from her pocket.

He looked on at her in disbelief. She had him speechless.

The most damaging thing Carmen had on him that he had no knowledge of, was the phone recording of the argument and shooting of Ralo, at the time they'd gone to confront him. She had everything on audio and stored on email to be used against him if need be. If only Reign Man knew the danger he'd called upon himself by not allowing Threat the opportunity to free him from that burden. The one he was to bear if and when Carmen was to go to the feds on him. Threat did, however, warn of that.

"So, you wanna tell me about this now?" She tried to urge him to be truthful.

"Huhhh!" he exhaled. "Look, Carm. Ok, you got it, all right? You win. What more could I say?" He finally gave in.

"But why, Vershon? That's all I want to know. Why? Out of all the bitches the great Reign Man could have and get pussy from, why fuck with my cousin? That's trifling as fuck, my nigga! Just low!" she let out.

I got weak, Carmen," he confessed. "She caught me in a vulnerable position and things took off from there."

Carmen gave him a condemning look. She was actually taken by surprise to hear him bring to the light what he concealed in the dark. There was now a need to question him a little further. She had to know what he was thinking.

"Vershon, why would you be so weak as to fuck with a careless bitch like Misty, that I got for a cousin? Huh? Please inform me. Why not some other female? I would've respected that more. Because I'm a real bitch. And I know not to trip because a nigga of your caliber wants an extra piece of pussy to go along with what he already have. That's a given. I know how to elevate above jealousy. But why that bitch? I could've considered a poly relationship, you know. With another female who's on the same level as I am. Or higher even," she stated to him. Those were her exact feelings.

"Like I said, she caught me in a vulnerable position. And it didn't hurt the fact that she does look like you in a lot of ways. She's got a body like yours and all. And she made me plenty of money. Money that you spend to enjoy the life you live," he responded. Another confession of the appealing qualities Misty utilized to seduce him.

Carmen gave him a blank look. There was no emotion there to express. She then decided to address his words in a way he least expected.

"Well, damn! Had I known all that, I would've let you have your cake and ice cream together, my nigga! Why didn't you say something? I probably would've thrown a piece of chocolate in the mix too, with Shug! It would've been you and three bad bitches, Vershon. But noooo! You just had to go about it in the wrong way, didn't you? And fucked up everything in the process," she stated emphatically to him. She shook her head in disgust once more.

"Ha! Just like that, you say?" Reign Man let out.

"No doubt. Just like that, playboy! And need I say again, you're Reign Man, the man, the myth and the legend. Why can't you have what you want? When you want it? And how you want it? Just like you had that night we met at the club on your birthday. You got who you wanted and what you wanted, right?"

"You right. You got a point there." He conceded to the logic Carmen laid out to him. "But Shug being in the mix. Nah, I couldn't do my nigga Breezy like that." He attempted to make humor, but Carmen found nothing funny.

"But you'll make it your business to do me that way, won't you?" she retorted.

He was made to shut the fuck up at that point.

Carmen added on to the point she was making. "Besides, had I been the one calling the shots on our private arrangement between you, me and whoever else, nobody but us would've known. Because I wouldn't be so stupid to post it on social media, unlike some other dumb bitch!" She spoke her raw truth.

"Well, what's done is done. And it's over with for that. I learned my lesson. And my intention is to do the right thing from here on out. Okay?"

"Just tell me this though. How long had your dealing with Misty been going on? When did it start?" Carmen wanted specifics.

"About a year. Maybe longer."

"So, basically from the time when she first got to Miami, huh?"

There was no need for him to think his way through the question. He didn't want to make an already bad situation any worse than it was. And the best thing he could do was not say a word more. That was the thing he'd done. Kept quiet.

Reign Man wanted to reconcile the differences they faced and move forward. However, Carmen was a woman scorned beyond repair. And her mind wasn't in the same space as his. Their vacation continued not so well.

***

The Miami FBI field office, located at 2030 SW 14th Avenue in Miramar, was contacted by an anonymous female caller. She was determined to make a report to them regarding a drug kingpin and his activities. Amongst other things, a murder as well that took place.

"FBI field office! How may I help you?" the female receptionist answered.

"Yes, I called because I would like to bring to your attention the ongoing drug dealing of an individual. And about a killing he committed as well. He's a dangerous person," the caller stated.

"Not a problem. Please hold while I direct you to the appropriate department, ma'am."

"Please do."

There was a pause that lasted roughly one minute. Classical music played while the caller was being transferred.

A special official then answered. "AUSA Kate Lindsey here."

"Yes, Miss Lindsey. I'm calling due to my grave concern for the safety and well-being of my female friend, it's her boyfriend who's the problem. He's a street drug kingpin."

"Okay. I'm more than sure we can help you with this. And just so you'll know, this call is being recorded," the prosecutor advised. "The information you provide shall be used as material to assist in any possible investigation that may come about."

"I don't have a problem with that. All I ask is that you help my friend, please."

"And we will. What's your friend's name?" the AUSA asked.

"Her name is Carmen. Carmen Margaux. That's M-a-r-g-a-u-x, Margaux. Her drug dealing boyfriend's name is Vershon Aikens. He goes by the street name of Reign Man. He forces her to do illegal things like traffic his drugs and other dirty deeds. Are you familiar with the names? Vershon Aikens? Reign Man?"

"We've heard the name a time or two before. But what else is going on between Aikens and Margaux?"

"He makes her launder money for him. The money he makes illegally." The caller began to cry at that point. She'd become emotional behind the thought of a person being shot and killed. She'd heard an audio recording of the entire incident.

The caller continued, "he told her if she doesn't do what he tells her to, or tries to leave him, he would surely kill her! And she's terrified of him."

"Ma'am, I promise you, we'll do the best we can to bring an end to the terror your friend is experiencing. Okay?"

"That's not all, ma'am. It gets worse."

"It does? How much worse?"

"A lot worse. My friend told me that a male cousin of hers, had a money dispute with the boyfriend, and the boyfriend pulled a gun and shot the cousin in the head, killing him!"

"Are you serious, ma'am?" asked the AUSA.

"Yes, ma'am. I am. The missing person, Chad Thompson aka 'Ralo,' that's the person who was killed. We don't know what was done with his body."

"Oh my! It was?" The federal official keyed in the name on her computer. She made quick notes of reference related to the information provided by the caller.

"We here at the FBI have been working hand-in-hand with the Miami Dade Police in our efforts to try and solve the disappearance of this particular guy. From what I recognize here on my computer."

"Well . . . he's dead."

"Ma'am, I have to ask. How long have you known this? It's policy that I ask."

"I didn't know until recently," the caller acknowledged.

"Is there more?"

"That's not enough?"

"Yes, it is. And we're going to look into all you've brought to our attention. I only asked in the event you had more to relate."

"Understood. But that's it. I'll call again if need be."

"Okay. And I'll be sure we make the appropriate steps regarding the matter. Thank you." The FBI official concluded the call.

***

Prior to the day, along with local authorities, the feds had already been provided a plethora of confidential information on the infamous Reign Man Aikens and his drug empire. However, the acts of murder hadn't gotten tossed into the equation. This raised the alarm, prompting action to be taken. An investigation ensued. This became the beginning of the end of the rule of Reign Man.

Seven

Reign Man and Carmen finally returned to the States. At times, she stayed at the home they once shared together, but mostly, at a hotel. At least until she'd been approved to move into an apartment she applied for. The plan was to move forward in life away from Reign Man as a single lady. This took place roughly two months after the anonymous caller contacted the FBI. The investigation intensified and turned up a treasure trove of evidence that could be used against both Reign Man and the girlfriend, Carmen.

It was easier to keep watch on Carmen and track her daily than it was regarding Reign Man. She was thoroughly photographed and her movement documented. The feds felt they had plenty to move in and make an arrest of her. They would then offer her a way out by way of informing on the boyfriend. They moved in to nab her. Her financial activity had a pattern to it. They'd pinpointed her next appointment at the OB/GYN.

***

A day following her arrest and signing of the cooperating agreement, Carmen was reunited with her daughter. The feds allowed her the opportunity to contact the babysitter, her sister, to arrange for them to meet at the airport. Carmen had orders not to make the sibling aware of what was going on, or the deal was off, and she'd be prosecuted on the indictment that had her listed on it. Carmen had a new status now and was a part of the government's Witness Protection Program.

To make matters more suitable for them, Reign Man was away on a so-called "business" trip to conduct deals for his product when they apprehended Carmen. This they knew. Travel data revealed a "Misty Margaux" booked a flight with a male, using the name "Demetrius Brown," en route to Las Vegas, Nevada. The Floyd Mayweather Jr. versus Manny Pacquiao boxing match was scheduled for that weekend. It was a Thursday. Courtesy of Carmen, the feds now knew who Misty was, and the alias of Reign Man.

Carmen and her daughter were already whisked away by the feds and sheltered at the training academy of the FBI, located in Quantico, Virginia. They had a duty to safeguard her until arrest and conclusion of trial for Reign Man. They patiently awaited his return home from his trip to Sin City. He would do so the following Tuesday. The arrest warrant was executed at that time.

Eight

Thirteen Months Later . . .

Vershon "Reign Man" Aiken's trial began. He had a nineteen-count indictment to contend against. Although he'd retained the best legal representation money could buy, the odds were stacked against him in a major way. The star witness for the government was yours truly, Carmen Jenine Margaux, aka "Caramel."

Throughout the weeks' long trial, Carmen was placed on the stand on three separate occasions, for both direct and cross examination by the AUSA who prosecuted the case, and Reign Man's defense team.

The jury heard detailed, yet damaging testimony against the defendant kingpin by the girlfriend. She related everything. She made the jury known of how the cousin Ralo was shot in the head and killed, without knowing exactly who pulled the trigger, due to having her head low from the effect of the beating Reign Man had laid on her. She related them to the jury as she had to the feds when they took her in. Reign Man was blamed and charged.

She related the incident about the mishap of hers regarding giving the wrong person the car that had fifteen kilos of narcotics stashed inside of it. About the beating perpetrated against her as an end result. She made it appear to the jury it was a brutal case of vicious violence he leveled upon her. The jury accepted her testimony.

The majority counts of the indictment were added, following the arrest of Reign Man and a search of his home.

They found military grade weapons, grenades, bulletproof vests and other body armor, in addition to three million in cash. No narcotics were discovered.

Numerous witnesses were called to testify. Even prior customers of Reign Man's, who'd previously bought his product. It didn't look good for the defendant at any time. The jury deliberated for five hours. They found Reign Man "Guilty" on all charges, with that of "Murder" topping the chart, conspiracy and RICO violations to follow.

Life as a free man was no more for the once mighty Reign Man. He was sentenced to life plus and shipped off to federal prison.

As for Carmen, the feds provided her a new identity and relocated her and Ni'Asia to Portland, Maine, to live out their lives under the Witness Protection Program.

Per government stipulations, Carmen, now going by "Charlotte Thorpe," was given strict orders to have absolutely no contact with anyone from her former life. Not even with her parents or any other family. Charlotte was a totally new person. "Carmen" had fallen from the ends of the earth. No one knew where she lived. No one saw her anymore nor heard from her again.

She had even gone so far as to have certain plastic surgery procedures performed to further alter her true identity. There was still a level of fear to her, and the threat of a potential hitman being hired by Reign Man to kill her. He had power and connections in the streets and money to advance any agenda he had in mind.

The feds didn't get all his money. And his heroin connection was still in place. Along with that of the meth supplier. He would continue to utilize them all throughout his doing time.

***

While in the state of Maine, Charlotte made a career in the medical field. She was educated and thoroughly trained in the profession, advancing from LPN to RN to NP.

Growing tired of the life lived in Maine and wanting to be around more African American colleagues and peers, Charlotte requested to be transferred. Her request was approved, and she was relocated to Washington, DC. She immediately acquired work at Med Star Washington Center Hospital. The nation's capital was now her and her daughter's residence. She'd lived in Maine for three years before transferring.

PART TWO

THESE VICIOUS STREETS | PRINCE A. TAUHID

Nine

Two Years Later . . .

Week-17 of the NFL football season, a divisional game was played between the Washington Redskins (at the time) and the Philadelphia Eagles. The battle was hosted in the City of Brotherly Love. A victory would grant either team a trip to the playoffs and the elimination of the other. Charlotte and her good friend Imani, a medical professional herself at the same hospital as Charlotte, attended the game to cheer on the Redskins, but also to party in Philly, as they had heard so much about the entertainment scene the city had to offer. The two had arrived the day before.

After the Eagles victory, there was to be a huge celebration at the Eagle Bar in North Philly on Erie and Germantown Avenues.

The head dude in charge over the event was a guy who so happened to have a hand in on the underworld of the city as well. His product of choice was heroin, and the territory he controlled was the part in north Philly called, "The Bad Lands."

The man of the hour developed a penchant that coincided with the street name he wore. He was born Barry Dean Murdoch, but better known and feared on the streets as "Murder." He'd made his bones and rose to the top under his cousin, a guy named Shepard Murdoch II. Murder put in dedicated work on the streets, had earned plenty of money pushing dope, and killed people who'd been ordered to die. His squad leader, Shepard, had the cousin do some of everything to advance the cause of the team. Murder proved to be a vicious and raw soldier.

Murder was in very good shape. He was above six feet tall and weighed two hundred and ten pounds. Based on his athletic abilities growing up, he loved to participate in sports. Boxing was his favorite. He loved to mix it up in the gym. Dude was brown-skinned in complexion, rocked a full one-inch beard, a *Philly beard* so to speak, and maintained a low-cut Caesar temp fade. Atop his well-groomed and charming gestures at times, he had the scariest features about himself. His pinkish lips were possibly the only easygoing trait about this north Philly monster the ladies he'd been with could attest to. The bottom line about Murder was he didn't play. He proved to be a hitter for real. And about rough action.

Opposite everything related to the notorious reputation Murder gained in the streets, there was another side to him. One too many people didn't know about, due to how quiet and private he was. He was a ladies' man, a gentleman, and a suave dude with a heart of gold regarding the females he dated, or the ones he found an attraction to. So, upon him having locked eyes with Charlotte at the post-game party of his, they both were able to charm and woo one another flirtatiously with body language and battling of eyes. Indeed, the opposites were able to attract in a compelling way.

The party was lit. Murder brought out all the big timers and playmakers of the city and surrounding locations, as the occasion was somewhat of a grand reopening of the bar under new management, "Murdoch Entertainment," a company he owned.

Murder found himself trying to transition from the relentless pressure associated with the mean and unapologetic duty required of him as a street don, to something more legit and less strenuous. He'd grown tired of continuing to take risks. Murder sought an exit strategy out of the game. He desired to stay alive and free.

Many came before him to make it to the top in street legend and lore. And at the same time, had disappeared as fast as arriving, either by death or with life in the feds. And at times, they'd disappeared without a trace. Murder didn't want to suffer the same devastating fate as his previous contemporaries and peers. There had to be an end game. A sustainable one.

***

Murder appealed to Charlotte more than Charlotte to him, for all the reasons she may have had in mind. She yearned for the many expensive accommodations that came along with being involved with a high-profile mature dope dealer, the likes of her ex, Reign Man Aikens. Murder resembled him in a lot of ways, only a brown-skinned version. But looks could be deceiving as often times was the case.

Murder got the attention of his sister Shaquana and called her over to have a word with him. She was younger than he was and was often utilized by Murder to communicate to other females the things her brother found interesting in them.

"Quana! Come here for a second," he said.

She was standing about ten feet away from him.

He kept his eyes locked on Charlotte.

Quana approached. "What's good, bro," she replied. "What's on your mind? Better yet, *who* you got on your mind? That's the better question."

She smiled at Murder, already half-knowing what he wanted. He returned a smile himself. They knew each other well.

"Her," he let out, pointing at Charlotte in a gesture. "Her right there. Shorty with the Versace outfit on."

Quana sucked her teeth from a spasm of envy that raced through her body at the sight of another female who was clearly her equal. She silently hated the fact of another female getting more attention than she was, even if it was from her brother. She threw the hate to the wayside once she came to realize that her brother exchanged side pieces like he does his underwear.

Quana spoke again. "What about her, bro? What about that hoe over there?" she playfully insulted.

"Don't be acting like you don't know what I want," Murder responded with a smile. "What I need you to do. I like what I see. Something different about her. She don't appear to be a Philly chick. That *jawn* there nice!"

"Um-hmm! Whatever. I see 'Miss Thotiana' got your attention! Let me go let her know my brother—the boss of these Philly streets—wanna have a word with her. And the bitch better not act all stank and shit either!" Quana declared.

"Look, just go let her know what's—"

Quana cut his words short. "Yeah-yeah, whatever. I'm just saying, bro." She then stepped off to go and take care of what her brother wanted her to do.

Quana had on a nice, fitted *Gucci* jumper. She looked just as stunning in appearance as Charlotte. She approached.

"Hey!" Quana greeted.

"Hello!" Charlotte replied.

"I'm Quana," she said, extending her hand to shake Charlotte's.

The day before, Quana had one of the best nail techs in all of Philly give her a mani and pedi. A nearly nine-hundred-dollar job. Charlotte took immediate notice of the high maintenance female in her presence. Quana gave off classy, sassy, and confident. All the things Charlotte had about herself was recognized in the other. Quana caused her to smile. They seemed to connect.

"Nice to meet you, Quana. I'm Charlotte."

"Nice to meet you too, Charlotte. But look, you see the fly guy standing over there? The one in the pink sweater?" She pointed in Murder's direction.

"I do. I noticed him the moment I walked in," Charlotte made her aware.

The friend, Imani, stood next to her and listened to the words exchanged.

"Well, that's a good thing. Makes my job a little more easy. I'm sure you already know the routine. What comes next, right?" Quana let out. She didn't beat around the bush.

"I've been through these type scenarios before. I know the drill," Charlotte declared with a smile. "Imani, sit tight for a moment, will you please? I'll be back shortly."

"No problem, girl. Do your thing. I'll step over to the bar and have a cocktail," Imani responded.

"I wouldn't mind having one myself," Quana chimed in. "You mind if I join you? Imani, right?"

"That's correct. And yes, you can join me. Let's do this."

Charlotte made her way towards Murder, sashaying through the crowd and drawing plenty of attention. She made it to his presence.

"Hey, pretty boy. How you? I was told you wanted to see me. I'm here," Charlotte said to Murder. Her level of confidence was next to the moon.

"What's poppin,' cutie? Yeah, I asked to see you. My attention was in your direction. So, what's your name?"

"I'm Charlotte. You?"

"I'm Barry, the man of the hour. Welcome to my party."

The two shook hands.

"Lucky guy. You always doing it big like this?"

"No doubt," he responded. His body language exuded confidence. She boosted his ego with the compliments.

"I work hard to have my way. It doesn't hurt to have a little luck to go along with it," he added.

"Hmmm. Interesting."

"I take it you're not from around here?"

"Nah, I'm not. Me and my friend visiting. Wanted to experience the club scene here in Philly. We're also huge

Redskins fans too. Went to the game today. We got a suite at the Marriott downtown."

"Huge Redskins fans!" Murder retorted. He wanted to show he had a sense of humor. He knew women loved that, especially in the first few minutes of meeting one another.

"You better not say that too loud around here, baby girl. Might cause you a few problems with us Eagles fans," he let out with a joking tone.

The witty flirtations continued.

"You appear to be the type of dude who knows how to deal with problems, Barry," she stated. Charlotte observed the security men Murder had surrounding him. Her words were a compliment.

"I see you observe well. I like that," he responded.

"I do. And I'm sure you won't let any problems come my way while I'm here on your turf as a fan. But a fan of two teams now. The Redskins, and the team you call the plays on," Charlotte stated. "Also, you may or may not believe it, but I'm currently a free agent. And looking to be picked up by someone who knows how to utilize the type of talent and skills I got."

Her confidence and the way she expressed herself appealed to Murder in a way like no other. The way she articulated, then made herself available, was an offer Murder simply couldn't pass up.

He continued to look upon her with a bright smile, chomping on his stick of Big Red chewing gum. His aura and mystique captivated Charlotte.

He spoke more. "Is that right? A free agent, huh? And what type of talent and skills you bring to the table? As you so gracefully put it."

"Ain't but one way to find out. And that has to be presented over time. In stages. And just so you know, if I do decide to date you, I'll have to be the main attraction. I don't do side show features. That's why I work so hard and maintain so well. To be the best version of myself, especially at the age I am."

"And what age is that?"

Charlotte then produced an elegant smile. It actually turned out to be a polite snub.

"Now-now, Barry, I'm sure you already know not to ever ask a lady what's her age. I'm gonna leave that for the imagination. But back to you. I like your style. I like the way you conduct and carry yourself in conversation."

"I like the same in you as well. You not some busted, bird-brain-having female looking to leech on a nigga."

"I'm absolutely not! On no level. I have too much respect and class about myself to do that."

"I can tell by the way you speak, you not some dumb uneducated broad either. That you do have a degree of learning. What you do for a living?" Murder asked.

"I'm a NP."

"NP!" he retorted, completely not knowing.

"Nurse Practitioner," she made him aware.

Charlotte then went on to relate to him her place of work.

"Gotcha on that. Sounds like a big title with big responsibility."

"The highest rank in nursing, one could say."

"Oh, yeah? Well, I definitely got to get to know more of you on a personal level. I need that special someone to help add real substance and merit to the paper I'm checkin' in. A nigga would like to change his life at some point. For the better, you know?"

Murder related a truth about himself he'd been holding in for quite some time.

"Life does have its ways of how it places two people in one another's lives at a time when transition may be needed," Charlotte responded.

"You couldn't have said it better. But this how I would like to do this, okay? I'mma leave you my number. And you be sure to hit me tomorrow, and make plans for a day when we might be able to meet again and really have a personal conversation. How that sound to you?"

"That'll be cool. I'm okay with it."

The two then exchanged information.

"I would stay and continue to have this conversation, but I got a little business to attend to. Just be sure to hit me up. And continue to be beautiful," Murder said. He then gently stroked Charlotte along her cheekbone, smiled, and then stepped away.

Truth be told, Charlotte could've been the feds for all he knew, someone on a special mission to infiltrate and tear down his organization. Although he deemed himself too street smart to allow his defense to break down behind a cute face and a banging body, dude had checks and balances in place to find out exactly who she really was, beginning the moment he had an opportunity to take her out. However, he did have her phone number. He could begin to dig in with that.

Ten

Murder was escorted by his bodyguards to his black-on-black 600-series Mercedes Benz, double parked in front of the bar. His best friend and right-hand man were there by his side. He was a dude by the name of Herbert Glover aka "Herb." The two hopped into the vehicle and began to make the ride to Bala Cynwyd, Pennsylvania, Lower Marion Township in Montgomery County. Murder had a nice low-key home there not too many people knew about. Only a handful. The two had business to deal with.

A half-hour later, they pulled into the home's garage. The electric door was lowered once more. The hundred-thousand-dollar luxury mobile was secured. The two got out. Instead of taking the stairway that led to the upper portion of the mini mansion, they took the one which led down into the basement. Two people awaited them. One was an early thirties hitter on Murder's team by the name of Traino. He was an executor to be reckoned with. His spirit was wraith-like. And the other person was a guy by the name of Montez Shaw, aka "Duck." He'd been duct-taped and tied down with a tight gag in his mouth. Duck turned out to be the only one not so fond of the meeting.

Prior to the day, Duck worked for Murder moving product. And then he found himself in trouble with Murder and the Philly Police Department. What happened was, Duck conspired with a cousin of his who did robberies on other drug dealers for a living. He was from South Philly. The plan was to hit one of Murder's stash spots. Everything went off smoothly, until Murder began to hear rumors circulating in the streets about the cousin bragging about how a cousin of his helped him pull off a caper of four kilos of heroin product.

Duck's name was mentioned. But, before Murder could get to him to question what he'd been hearing, Duck ran to the Philly PD drug task force for help. He was nowhere to be found. While snitching to the cops on the things he knew about Murder, the Homicide Division was provided an earful by Duck as well. He felt the need to air out all his dirty laundry.

Days before the stick-up by Duck and his people, Duck pulled a foul move against Murder to try and have him out the way to make it easier for them to hit other spots. In addition, he'd secretly recorded Murder on the phone as he did a drug transaction.

While riding along with Murder one day to be resupplied with product, Murder had other customers and workers to supply as well, as the same time as Duck. It was a Thursday—the day most retail spots normally were provided packages. Murder handed Duck a quarter-kilo of heroin and had him exit the car and deliver the package to a cousin of his who was waiting inside the house. Duck made sure to be way chatty in both instances, while he was in the house passing off to the family member of Murder, Cortino. Duck made it his business to become an informant on his own accord. Snitching for the fuck of it, an effort to advance his plan to rob.

Murder and Cortino were eventually arrested after the house was raided by the drug task force. The video Duck provided helped to have a warrant issued. Not to mention, the ounces of heroin the cops found in the spot. Bail was posted. Between arrest and Motion for Discovery being provided to show the video and exactly who the rat turned out to be, Duck and his people hit a couple of spots that belonged to Murder. Duck then ran back to Philly PD for protection afforded to a C.I.

Murder had a brother who was a law enforcement official. He worked as a drug task force agent. His name was Jabari Murdoch. He and Murder had the same father. Not too many people knew of this. Jabari brought it to Murder's attention that his name was being tossed around in various divisions of the department a little more than it should have. He told him specifically who the snitch was. A photo was provided as well, along with an address on where to locate Duck.

Murder sent Traino to track down Duck, take him hostage, and hold him in place in the basement of the home until he arrived. The day the Eagles advanced to the playoffs was a good time to do so. All the attention of the cops was placed on events after the game.

Murder and Herb approached Duck, who was chained and looking like an animal in the basement.

"Hot damn, Duck!" Murder let out.

Duck was bleeding from the head and squirming about on the concrete floor. Traino had put a mean beat-down on him.

"I never would've thought it was you who sold me out to the cops, then turned and robbed my spots. You ratted for no reason. Then you continued on with being a C.I., looking to be protected by the police. How did that work out for you?" Murder taunted.

Duck tried to word something in defense of himself. "The cops forced me to try and say something to them about you."

"Yo, bro, take that from his mouth for me so I can hear what type of bullshit he's put together to tell me," Murder said to Traino. He was in the mindset to believe Duck would tell who was in with him to rob his trap spots.

"Now, what was that? I didn't hear you that well the first time."

"I said, the cops tried to force me to tell them whatever it was I may know about you. But I didn't."

The three friends looked at one another with confused expressions. They knew Duck was lying out the ass.

"What the fuck you mean by that! And how the fuck Philly PD get you in that kind of situation anyway?"

"I went to them, bro. But not about you. One of my crazy cousins took my daughter and threatened to kill her if I didn't do what he told me to do."

"You mean do what he told you to do, like set up my people at my spots to be robbed and shot, right?" Murder got straight to the point.

"Basically, that's the part I was getting to," Duck responded.

"Who this 'crazy cousin' of yours you talkin' bout?" Murder demanded to know.

"That nigga, Elze. My so-called people from S.P.," Duck provided a name.

"Elze!" Murder retorted. He and his guys never heard of dude before. But he wanted to get to the bottom of it.

"Yeah, he's a stick-up kid. He loves to rob dope boys," Duck let out in a whimper of breath. He was weak. The heavy beating had taken a toll.

"So, let me get this straight. This cat Elze came to you about robbing my spots, because he knew you worked for me. Then, you refused. So, he took your daughter and threatened to kill her if you didn't? You then ran to the cops. But instead, they questioned you about me in the process, and both my spots still got robbed. And I assume you got your daughter back, because I ain't seen nothing on the news about a little girl being killed. And then, you still end up quacking to the cops about my business. But what about the video you recorded on your phone that day I had you with me, and I had you deliver that work to my people, Cortino? You wanna tell me about that? We got booked behind that. And you can't make up some bullshit to feed me on that either, nigga!" Murder barked. He sneered in Duck's face. He then squatted low to reveal what he knew.

"Video recording on my phone?" Duck retorted. He was shocked to know Murder now knew of his activities as a C.I. "What video?"

"Nigga, don't play dumb on me! What the fuck wrong with you, Duck? You should've known I was gonna find out about that shit!" Murder spat vehemently.

I wonder how the fuck this nigga know about that? Duck thought. *Philly PD was supposed to have kept that confidential.* So, he thought.

"Yo, Murder. Word to my mama, bro, I ain't rat you out to the cops!" Duck attempted to lie his way out of the situation.

Murder walked over to the corner area of the basement. He had his sporting equipment stationed there. In particular, a set of golf clubs. He pulled one from the bag. It was a 9-iron. He then slowly walked back to where Duck was positioned and took a stance over his head. It was as if he was about to tee off for a hole-in-one.

"You say 'word to your mama, you ain't rat me out to the cops, right?" he asked of Duck, then shuffled his body and evened out his feet. He balanced himself.

"Word to my mama, bro! What I gotta do to prove it?" Duck asked. He now panicked like crazy. His heart damn near pounded out his chest.

Murder paused before responding, "You say what you gotta do to prove it? How about . . . die for the shit you did, then come back as a real nigga!" he spat, then drew back the club as far as he could for a swing.

Whop!

He connected squarely on the side of Duck's head. Right on the ear.

Whop! Whop!

He worked him twice more for good measure.

Duck's face and head were severely disfigured. He was dead as ever. No longer able to quack the police about Murder, or squeal on any other activities he knew about.

Murder then ordered his two homies to take Duck's body and dump him in the large plastic tank he had on hand once they ripped his clothes off. The tank was full of powerful acid, designed to eat up and dissolve the flesh of dead animals, or any stubborn raw sewage or other bio-hazardous material.

It was now on to the next one, locate the Elze dude Duck made mention of, then end his days of living. Murder sent Traino out on the job. He would also have Jabari pull up his profile and provide any information he could find on him. The war continued.

Eleven

Murder and his sister Quana got together to take a trip to Annapolis, Maryland, to visit someone they both were very familiar with. It was their mother, Karen. She'd long gotten her life back on the right track, after many years of being hooked on heroin, while living in her hometown of Philadelphia, PA.

Karen is the twin sibling to a brother. Murder couldn't stand his uncle due to his inability to get clean himself and out the streets. He still roamed the hood of North Philly and held zero plans to walk a straight line and free himself of dope addiction. The uncle's name is Kevin. He and Karen had the same last name, Fredricks. But Kevin was known by all as "Dollar Bill."

The twins used to rip and run the streets together, getting high and doing damn near everything under the sun to support their habit. These were the days long before "Barry" made a name for himself in the streets to become "Murder." And a time when the youngster took out his anger and rage on others, behind the hurt and the pain of not having his mother to care after him and his sister. Murder was too embarrassed and ashamed of Karen to be seen at school or elsewhere with her and had to fight daily behind the insults he experienced. At times, two to three times daily against the other hoodlums around his age who would pick at his mother endlessly. Murder later took all ill matters into his own hands and treated any form of disrespect with a severe penalty, thus earning the name and reputation he so proudly wore with no remorse.

It turned out to be Murder's decision to force his mother into the rehab program in Maryland, one of the best in country at treating heroin addiction, away from Philly and the bad influences. And especially away from her twin dope head brother, Dollar Bill. Murder hated that nigga with a passion. But respected him only because he was family.

Murder also knew it was important to have his mother out of harm's way to prevent any would-be threats from coming to her from enemies, in their attempts to get at him. Although Karen was a dope fiend momma and not much of a pretty sight to the eyes any longer, her son still had compassion and love for her to not allow the streets to swallow her whole. Murder wouldn't allow any casualties of war to befall him and his family. No matter how hooked on dope they may be. And that even included his uncle who he hated, Dollar Bill. He knew how much his mother loved her twin. And Murder promised her he'd look after him. He put it on his soul.

Karen had a nice townhouse in Annapolis. It was fully paid for by Murder. She and her boyfriend lived together. He was a guy twelve years her senior. They hooked up at the rehab center they both graduated from. He was a white dude by the name of Randle. They were happy together. This affair turned out to be all Murder and Quana wanted for their mother, love, peace, and happiness. Her white intimate companion, Randle, provided this for her.

Murder and Quana took one of his low-profile cars for the trip. He felt the need to keep being discreet and not draw any attention to them. He didn't want any high-level dealers in the city to get the wrong impression that some Philly cat was there putting it down on their turf, and his mom's house was the trap spot. Not that Karen and Randle lived in a neighborhood where that type of action was going on. It's that there are certain types of street dudes everywhere, and often times, get things twisted. And a war could potentially start by someone misjudging.

The two siblings arrived at their mother's house and entered. She was happy to see them physically. It had been two long months.

"There goes Momma's two babies," Karen said joyously. She smiled brightly at the sight of her children, displaying those near perfect dental implants of hers. Murder paid a grip to have the procedure performed. Heavy drug use and neglect from street life had done a number on Karen's natural teeth.

"Hey, Momma!" Quana was the first to respond. She hugged Karen and pecked her about the cheekbone.

"Hi, Mom!" Murder next spoke. "How you been, baby? What up, Randle! Everything good?" He then greeted the boyfriend. They both gave Randle a hug as well. He'd been busy watching the playoffs. It was the divisional round of the tournament.

Randle stood at six foot seven. He wore a goatee, a Marine crew-cut hairstyle, and was of average build. He had a slight pot belly from the many home cooked meals Karen prepared. And he was the type of guy who loved to preoccupy himself with anything regarding science fiction, tattoos, and gadgets. His duties in the military were science, engineering and technology. Randle adored Pop-science magazines and books. Especially those by the author, Harlan Ellison.

"I'm doing well, Barry. Me and your mother. How you and your sister been?" Randle responded.

"We been good. Can't complain."

"Yeah. We doing good, Randle. Thanks for asking," Quana chimed in to say.

They all took a seat in the living room on the couch to tune in to the football game. Randle loved the Baltimore Ravens. His hometown team. Karen had Sunday dinner going for them. Murder and Quana had good timing. They definitely wanted to eat.

"So, what made you two want to surprise me with a visit?" Karen asked.

Quana kept quiet and allowed Murder to answer up on that. It was his plan after all.

"Actually, we had intentions to go and see someone else today. They don't live too far away from y'all neck of the woods, over in DC. A female I met."

"Oh! You got a nice young lady who got your attention, huh? You say she live in DC? When you plan to bring her by to let Momma meet her?"

"We just met not too long ago, Mom. Let me properly vet her first. Then we'll get to that part. I promise you on that," Murder related to his mother. He now had a shy smile.

"Well, how she look? And what she do for a living?" Karen dug in.

She then took a look at Quana for answers. She knew her baby was always eager to spill the tea.

"How she look, Quana?" Karen asked with a smile. "What's your take on this kitty who got the attention of that bobcat you got for a brother?"

Quana construed her face and sucked her teeth. The thought of Charlotte compelled her to keep in mind the stiff level of competition she presented. In a good way though.

Karen spoke up once more. "I mean, she's got to be somebody special for your brother to make it his business to drive hours to see her. In addition to seeing us."

"She a'ight, Mom. Kinda too *bougie* for me. But those the type of jawns bro go for. So, I guess she's cool. She didn't come off any type of ill way. But that could be a front she putting on to catch my brother." Quana gave her opinion. "By the way, her name is Charlotte. Reminds me of the children's story you use to read to me, *Charlotte's Web*, about the female spider that had others caught up over her. Or something like that. I can't quite remember," she added with a smile and a touch of sarcasm.

Karen smiled, then turned back to look over at her son. She rubbed him on the head and gave him a few words to think over about the potential girlfriend.

"Well, Barry, if you like her and how things have begun between you two, then continue to go for her. Just be sure to bring her by soon, so your momma can read her. Okay?"

"No problem, Momma. I got you," Murder responded.

They all talked a bit longer until the food was ready. Murder and Quana ate with their mom and the boyfriend.

It was time to leave at that point and head to the nation's capital. Murder wanted to pull up on Miss Charlotte Thorpe on a surprise visit as well. The time reached 5:00 p.m. Charlotte's work shift began at 3:00. Throughout the few times they talked on the phone, she made him aware of this.

***

The sibling duo pulled into DC's city limits. They then made their way to the medical facility where Charlotte practiced, via GPS. He remembered the name of the facility she mentioned.

Days before, Murder contacted the Medical Center to verify if she had told him the truth about where she worked. She was honest. Something he'd already felt, but simply had to confirm. Her title and position turned out to be the truth as well. It was her honesty, that really had Murder thoroughly pursuing her as no other female he had before. He really took a liking to Charlotte. However, his sister Quana wasn't too fond of the other sexy feline for whatever her reasons were. Quana's female intuition wouldn't allow her to settle on Charlotte so fast, although she had the brother's undivided attention.

To Quana, there was more to Charlotte she concealed behind her chuckle and the twinkle of her eye. It made Quana suspicious. Like Charlotte had something she was hiding. A possible ugly reality that was ebbing below the surface. The naked eye couldn't see it. This became the main reason why Quana wanted to tag along with her brother to meet Charlotte again, to find out more about who the *real* Charlotte was.

Other than that, Quana liked the girl and wanted to know more about her personally, to establish a bond they could benefit from, being Quana already silently envied Charlotte's style and polished sex appeal that came along with her. Quana felt she could utilize some of what Charlotte had to balance out the bad girl mentality and rough edges the ghettos of Philly made her into. Quana desired a transformation. She wanted to move away from sneakers and Timberland boots, to heels and flats. From jeans and sweats, to cocktail dresses and other formal attire that was more lady-like.

By the way, *"every lady is a woman, but every woman is not a lady."* Quana once heard before and wanted to be enlightened on the difference between the two. Her street thug boyfriend always stressed this philosophy to her at every opportunity he had. And Quana took notice that Charlotte knew a lot about this particular truth.

Once they entered the hospital, the two approached the reception desk. Murder had a few gifts on hand to treat the apple of his eye.

"Hello, may I help you?" the petite, brown-skinned African American professional asked of them.

"Yes, yes you may. We're here to see a Charlotte Thorpe, please. NP Charlotte Thorpe, that is," Murder stated.

"Miss Thorpe? Sure, no problem," the receptionist responded.

Murder caught on to something. The way the receptionist put a handle on things.

"I noticed you spoke her name proudly, ma'am," he said.

"That's because Miss Thorpe has made quite a name for herself here, sir. She's an honored professional in many medical circles." She piled on the compliments.

"That's good to know."

The call for Charlotte was then made over the PA system.

"NP Charlotte Thorpe, please contact the main lobby! NP Charlotte Thorpe, please contact the main lobby!"

Shortly thereafter, the phone at the desk buzzed.

"Main lobby, April here," the receptionist answered.

Apparently, Charlotte was on the opposite end of the phone.

"Yes, Miss Thorpe. You have a couple of people here to see you, ma'am," she made her aware. "I'll let them know," another reply, then a pause. "Bye-bye," April lastly stated into the phone. "Miss Thorpe says she'll be here shortly," she relayed to Murder. Quana continued to keep silent.

"Thank you, ma'am," he graciously responded.

Shortly, Charlotte made it from the fourth floor, down the elevator, down a short stretch of hallway, and into the lobby to be greeted by a smiling Murder and his sister. He was holding a dozen long-stem red roses in one hand and a greeting card with pink ribbon attached, and in the other, a box of expensive chocolate.

"Well, hello to you, Charlotte! How you been?" Murder said to her.

The look of surprise Charlotte had about her face was priceless.

"Yeah. Hey, Charlotte! How you been?" Quana chimed in to say. She had a smirk about her face.

"Well, oh . . . hello, there . . . ah . . . you two. I've been good. Wasn't expecting to see you two on such short notice. But nonetheless, you're here." Charlotte said. Her smile was a welcoming bright one.

"That's correct. We're here. Bearing gifts and the whole nine for you, Miss Lady." Murder put on his charm and extended the offering to Charlotte. She gladly accepted.

April looked on in admiration.

"So, what brings you two here?" Charlotte asked.

"That's an easy one. I wanted to see you. I remembered the name of this hospital here. And like I told you before, I love to be spontaneous at every chance I can. So, I figured, why not hit the road and come to DC to check you out?" Murder responded to her.

"I did mention to you where I worked, didn't I? This is a good time, and a not so good time," Charlotte put out there.

"Why the 'not so good time'?" he questioned.

"Well, to be specific, I have to work a sixteen-hour shift. And, I wish I had the time off today to treat you two to a nice time here in DC. But unfortunately, I'm unable to," Charlotte explained.

"Oh. That part. And here it was, I was looking forward to us doing something fun together," Quana said.

"I really wish I could . . . um . . . Quana."

Quana smiled. "I see you remembered my name. That's a good thing," Quana said. She had an intense gaze locked on Charlotte.

"Yeah, I remembered. How could I forget? I left Philly knowing only two names of the people I encountered."

"Barry and Quana," Quana blurted.

"That's right," Charlotte remarked. "But hey, I'm off all next weekend. Will you two be able to come back then?"

"I'm a boss, Charlotte, and a CEO. I make my own hours. Of course, I will for you. Anytime," Murder boasted with a smile. "But when I do, I want to spend the whole weekend with you. All to myself. How that sound?"

"That's a possibility. Just hit me up Thursday to let me know when you'll be here. And I'll text you my address then. Okay?"

"Sounds like a plan to me," Murder accepted her offer.

"Sounds like one to me as well, Barry," Charlotte lastly said. She gave Murder a hug, Quana a handshake and wished her visitors well-being before heading back to her work area. She held a lot of responsibility on the fourth floor of a busy hospital.

The brother and sister duo left out, satisfied with the results to have come about with their surprise visit.

Quana was happy for her brother. More at the fact that he pursued someone who made him smile, and someone who brought out the gentleman he had in him. If only she could get him to help her in this area now. That would be better. But the problem was that Murder didn't know what Quana had an appetite for. She never really made her sexual orientations known. *Bisexual maybe?* So thought Murder. Being she did have a boyfriend to fulfill the urge she had every so often. And possibly a girlfriend, for all Murder knew. But the way she put it to him was that she had a hard time finding a dude who was rugged and mentally tough enough to handle her in the way she needed to be handled.

I may have to find somebody for Quana's hard to deal with ass at some point soon. She seems to be jealous of the appearance and success Charlotte has, Murder thought over his observance of how his sister looked upon and spoke to the female he pursued.

Twelve

Four Days Later . . .

Murder was back on the road headed to DC to meet with Charlotte and to spend time. He was alone. In his Benz. His security men had instructions to follow him out of Philly to the Pennsylvania and Delaware state line. That was to ensure no one followed. No enemies or potential hostage takers looking to get a king's ransom. Once Murder reached the point where he felt safe, the bodyguards were to turn and go back to Philly to hold down the fort with his uncle Odell (his dad's brother). Murder had plans to be away four days.

Murder didn't mention anything to anyone about where he was going or when he was to return. However, his sister Quana knew from the previous trip the two took. And the notes Murder had her to make in her phone to remind him Charlotte was off for the weekend that was to come.

Quana, being the type of female she turned out to be, ran her mouth a little too much to the boyfriend in her life about how much she didn't like Charlotte, and about how much she actually did adore the style and class she had. Her feelings of Charlotte were contradictory to one another. Amongst the thought of how much she couldn't stand how some random chick had her brother's nose wide open, and how the female had Murder paying top dollar for expensive roses, chocolate and greeting cards.

The boyfriend, Raheem Jones, aka "Heeme," was a dude Murder knew little to nothing about. Quana kept him private. So was the relationship they had, for all intents and purposes.

Heeme was two years younger than Quana. He was a youngster who had extraordinary swag, a bad-boy attitude, and mystique to control and manipulate Quana the way he saw fit. She found herself obsessed with dude. And to satisfy his every want and every need, Quana did any and everything he wanted to keep dude happy and interested in her. Heeme had his way.

The pillow talk between Quana and Heeme turned out to be more fulfilling for him than the sex before it. He liked Murder. And at the same time, he hated him for all the reasons he felt he should hate him, jealousy and envy, basically, due to how cocky and arrogant Murder had the tendency to be. Anytime he flexed his muscle and power in the streets, a lot of niggaz feared Murder. And also, there were a lot of cats who didn't. Heeme was one of those die-hard, bar-none type of young dudes. He would bust his gun at the snap of a finger to prove it.

As far as the relationship between Quana and Heeme, he ensured she kept things on the low between them, as he didn't want or need Murder in their business, trying to dictate to his girl what she could or couldn't do. Not to mention, whom she should or shouldn't date.

Heeme committed high level robberies on dope boys who had it. Weight dealers. And he knew that wouldn't sit well with Murder, had he found out. Heeme also had maintained in mind that he would rob Murder too, once he got close enough or caught him slipping down bad. If any conflict were to potentially arise between the two—Heeme and Murder—Heeme was already on his brother's team, and his street squad posed as an op to Murder and his crew. So, he had back-up.

Quana spoke all about her and her brother's trip to DC. About Charlotte as well. How they met, what Murder told her he'd like to have with her, and to what extent he was willing to go to know the sexy nurse. She ended by revealing Murder was to travel to DC again at 10:00 a.m. that

Thursday, the day that was upon them. Heeme jumped at the opportunity to at least know where Murder would potentially be stashing money and drugs in the weeks to come. Heeme also came to realize he had to be calculated in any method of attack he had in mind. And that was what he'd done.

Heeme got a head start on Murder that day. He hit the road himself about an hour early, at 9:00 a.m., so to pull alongside the road in Delaware just outside of Wilmington. He made it appear that his car was broken down and needed to be towed. The plan was to lay and wait for Murder to pass, then hop in behind him all the way to DC. He knew what Murder's favorite vehicle looked like, and also knew more than likely the Benz would be the car he took. It had a chrome license plate at the front that had the words "PHILLY'S FINEST," a distinguishing item to help Heeme know the car belonged to Murder. The phrase on the name plate referred to the entertainment brand Murder was building with his record label. Nonetheless, a dead giveaway to identify the owner of the car.

The moment of truth arrived. Heeme's patience paid off. In his rearview, he took notice of a vehicle that fit the description of Murder's. It was approaching at a cruising speed. The closer the car got, the more Heeme knew. In passing, the plate was recognized. Heeme had confirmation.

"There you go. Gotcha!" Heeme worded to himself.

It was no doubt, Murder behind the wheel.

Heeme allowed Murder to get about forty car lengths, then he hopped in the long line of traffic that was traveling that day. He kept a sharp eye on the Benz ahead of him. There was a good idea Murder wouldn't make any stops along the way. And no need to trail too closely. He didn't want to give his target any reason to believe he was being followed.

Hours later, the intense 'cat and mouse' chase came to an end at a modest home situated in the Trinidad section of DC. Murder reached his destination, parked out front of the house, got out and walked up to the door. Heeme was sure to bring along a small digital camera and a pair of powerful military grade binoculars. He bought them from a surplus store on Germantown Avenue and 6th Street in Philly.

Heeme took a lot of pictures of the home, the car in the driveway, other surroundings, and wrote down the address he noticed on the brick mailbox.

No sooner had he arrived, Heeme then vanished the same, on his way back to Philly to put together a potential plot he could put into play to extort Murder. He now had a degree of leverage.

***

Charlotte opened the door to let Murder inside. He was the first to speak behind the pleasing smiles they gave one another.

"Well, well, well. If it ain't my female infatuation standing in front of me once more. Hey, Charlotte! How you been? I'm here in DC once more." His smile was maintained.

"I see. This is a very good thing. And I'm happy to see you, Barry," Charlotte responded.

The two hugged and she welcomed him inside.

"Nice car you have. Very nice," she commented. "You're dressed nice as well."

"Thank you. You look nice yourself. I look forward to making this a weekend to be remembered."

"Me as well," she remarked.

A moment later, a little girl appeared from the back room of the house. She wanted to see who the man was who drove the nice car parked out front of their home. She'd taken a look out the window. The young one stood in silence and looked on at the handsome man who stood present and speaking with her mother. She immediately took notice of the way her mom smiled and marveled at the guy. She smiled to herself at the sight. The mother hadn't smiled that way in a long time. The eight-year-old knew this.

"And hello to you too," Murder greeted the little girl.

Charlotte then turned and took notice of her daughter standing at a distance.

"Hi!" the little one responded.

"Oh. That's Ni'Asia. My daughter," Charlotte made him aware.

"Ni'Asia, huh? She's beautiful. Just like her mother." He turned his charm on.

"Ni'Asia was about to be picked up by Imani to go spend the weekend with her daughter, Farrah. But it looks like she won't be going because she's not dressed and not gonna be ready by the time Imani gets here to take her with them! Now will you, Ni'Asia?" Charlotte playfully threatened. "And this is Barry, Ni'Asia. Now go get ready to leave. Auntie Imani will be here shortly."

"Imani? That's the friend who was with you that time in Philly, right?"

"Yep. That's her," Charlotte confirmed. "We both have a daughter near the same age. They do almost everything together."

Murder smiled at the thought of the two little girls enjoying life growing up together. The thought of his daughter then passed through his mind. She was only four at the time cancer took her precious life. Leukemia. That was five years prior to the day.

"I had a daughter," he uttered. Charlotte caught on to the use of a past-tense word he had let out. "Had."

"What happened?" she asked.

"Leukemia. Almost five years ago."

"I'm sorry to hear that, Barry." She offered a word or two to help comfort behind the thought.

"Thanks."

The two then took a seat and began a conversation. Imani finally pulled up to get Ni'Asia. No sooner afterwards,

Murder and Charlotte were out, gone about their business for a night out on the town. He'd already booked a suite at the Ritz-Carlton Hotel for the weekend as his plan was to not leave until Monday came.

The first stop made by the two was to a dinner party Charlotte was invited to, plus one. It was hosted by a well cultivated colleague of hers. The theme was a black-tie event. Murder was made aware of the occasion a day before and was dressed accordingly.

While there at the affair, Charlotte played her part to the tee. She introduced Murder to the many she knew from work. She made it appear as if the two had been in a relationship for years leading to the day. It was like their reality were as if she'd taken a major chance on dude, and she was overly determined to make it work at all costs.

The truth of the matter was the day Murder and Quana pulled up on Charlotte at the hospital and he had those gifts, she utilized the opportunity superficially in the eyes of those who looked on as she was charmed by the handsome guy who blessed her. The receptionist, April, spread the word herself in a crazy way about the happy visit. When Charlotte returned to the floor she worked on, carrying her romantic articles of affection, the African American female doctor she worked under, admired heavily and then offered the invite to her event, the "Black Tie" gala and fundraiser they now attended. Murder was being used in a good way, whether he took notice or not.

The doctor approached the two. "So, this is who the announcement over the PA system for you was all about? You had a special male visitor, I see. How nice of him to give you those gifts," Doctor Henderson stated. Her compliment was genuine.

Charlotte wanted so badly to be part of the circle of elite medical professionals led by Doctor Henderson. No matter how she was granted access, she wanted in, even if that meant at the expense of Murder. It mattered not to her. The perfect timing of Murder turned out to be the golden ticket to grant her entrance.

While toasting glasses of expensive champagne, sipping casually, Charlotte's acquaintance with Doctor Henderson gained strength. Laverne Henderson was pleased with the progress being made by her.

"Hello, Doctor Henderson!" Charlotte fawned. "How are you, ma'am? Me and Barry wanted to thank you dearly for your invite to this fabulous event. We can't thank you enough."

If "fake it until you make it" was an actual person, Charlotte was the poster girl for the phrase. She knew how to master the moment.

"You're welcome, Charlotte. You really are," responded the dark, smooth-skinned, natural hair wearing ultra professional.

Doctor Henderson fit the look as if she belonged on the TV show, *Married to Medicine*.

Charlotte nudged Murder in the ribs with her elbow gently while Doctor Henderson briefly looked away. She needed him to speak, to at least show what level of class and articulation she knew he had. He got the hint.

"Yes, Doctor Henderson. Thank you again for having us here at your affair," the street don expressed. "How may we show our gratitude and appreciation?"

"He's so gracious and charming, Doctor Henderson. He truly is," Charlotte chimed in to say to add a heightened element to the facade she was putting on.

"I see. He's a man of charm and manners," declared Doctor Henderson.

"Yes, ma'am, he is," Charlotte cosigned then smiled. She looked from Doctor Henderson to Murder then back again. "Also, Doctor Henderson, Barry and I wanted to know how we may show our appreciation for you being so kind to welcome us to your event?"

Although this was the first time Charlotte attended an affair Doctor Henderson hosted, she'd heard many times the

THESE VICIOUS STREETS | PRINCE A. TAUHID

elder professional had a charity foundation, and anyone who put any money towards it, would most certainly earn an honorable mention to the many other folks of upper echelon in the medical society. This night would be an opportunity for Charlotte to establish her name with those she looked up to.

Doctor Henderson spoke again. "Well . . . generous donation to a cause I'm in support of is always a good way to show appreciation, Charlotte," she stated.

Charlotte took a look into the eyes of Murder. Her smile was illuminated. She knew from the evening in Philly at the event he'd hosted, that he kept large amounts of cash on his person at any time he felt the need to feel important.

Charlotte had a question. "Doctor Henderson, does any of the non-profits you've founded contribute to fighting cancer and the research thereof?"

She touched on the issue she knew Murder wouldn't have a problem pouring money into, now that she knew cancer took the man's daughter.

"Absolutely there is. Absolutely," replied Doctor Henderson.

Charlotte turned and took a deeper look into the eyes of Murder once more, but with a sympathetic disposition about her face now. He then pulled out a thick roll of cash.

"Will a cash donation suffice, ma'am?" Charlotte asked.

"Charlotte! Honey! In America, the Beautiful . . . cash is king!" Doctor Henderson stated in a concluding manner. "If you will, you two just head right on over to the donation booth to take care of things. And I'll be sure to add the names of you both to the list of honorable mentions to be announced tonight. That's Charlotte Thorpe and gentleman Barry, correct?"

"That's correct, ma'am," responded Charlotte.

She and Murder then made their way across the room and reported to the donation window.

Murder had twenty thousand in his possession. He peeled off one hundred and fifty hundred-dollar bills and handed it over to the teller of the booth. A teardrop slowly rolled down his face, obviously cherishing the memory of his beloved little girl, Bethany. He was provided with a receipt. The two then continued about the night at the affair.

Thirteen

Murder and Charlotte took it in for the night at the hotel suite he'd reserved. Smooth music played at a low volume. Scented candles burned. The lights were dimmed. And the two enjoyed a bottle of Chardonnay as they held a conversation to reveal more of themselves personally. They were now in cozy sleepwear. He had on a pair of tiger striped silk boxers and a tank top, while she seduced in a matching set of cherry red thongs and a bra. Murder loved to get his mind right and brought along an ounce of strawberry Kush to blow on over the weekend.

"So Barry, tell me, because I'm curious to know," Charlotte gave a prop to the question she had in mind.

"What's that, babe?"

"I know I'm a nice-looking woman and all that. And I know I've got a nice body. Along with the qualities about myself to make any man worthy to get in the pursuit of me. But what was it about me that made you want to get to know me?" she asked a two-fold question.

Murder let out a thick cloud of weed smoke. He then hit his drink, pinched his nose, and took a snort before offering a reply.

"It was because . . . I had a good idea you was different than all the others. I took notice you wasn't from Philly. And you just had a certain type of vibe and glow about yourself that said 'class and taste.' I simply had to take my best shot. And I scored. I love to win at any game I'm in. Ain't no doubt about that," Murder stated. His level of confidence was to the moon like most often times.

Charlotte pursed her lips, furrowed her eyebrows, and slowly raised her head in acknowledgement. She admired his compliments. They seemed poetic. Her soul became infatuated with his world.

"Is that right," she sensually uttered. She then eased closer to plant a tender kiss on his neck. Then his lips.

"And when I made it my business to fact check you with everything you provided me about you, that really made the little motor of my heart go."

"How so? What did you discover?"

"Look, I'mma street nigga, Charlotte. Always have been, and probably always will be. I don't know how much of the streets you can relate to. But my point is that I don't ever get the 'God-honest truth' out of people on a regular. If ever any truth at all! So, for you to relate yourself to me and not lie, that said a lot about you as a person. And I had to at least pull up on you in a surprise visit with those gifts I gave. By the way, Quana suggested that'll be a good thing. A 'wise thing' as she put it. The element of surprise is a play that can be used for many valuable reasons."

He so eloquently placed his words in context.

Charlotte looked him square in the eyes. She then let out a slight chuckle at the comments he made. He was completely oblivious of her true history. There was no way he could find that part out.

"What's funny?" he had to ask with a smile about his face.

"I'm laughing at you. But in a good-natured way though. What makes you think I don't know anything about the streets? Or about the products that get sold in the streets?" she asked.

"Charlotte, I don't see not one stain of street smart on you. And I mean nowhere. I don't see nothing about the streets associated with you. Besides, you too damn honest! Ain't no honest motherfuckas' in the streets! Period! It's a blood sport out there! No love! No glory! It is what it is," Murder spat.

He then pointed his finger as he spoke to indicate the world at large. His emphasis was understood by her.

"And you really think that? That I don't know nothing about the streets?"

"Ah, yeah. That's exactly what I think. Duh!" he confirmed his take on her. "However, if you do, give me a little-known history of your struggles in the streets?" Murder requested.

The immediate thoughts of the life once lived with Reign Man came to mind.

Do I say anything? Or do I continue to keep him in the blind? she thought.

She felt comfortable to open up a little. Just a little.

"Well, look. Here's the deal . . . *Murder*." She called him by his street name. It was spoken at the party in Philly. She startled him with it. He jumped and jarred his head at the same time.

Charlotte continued. "I came to this country at an early age. I transitioned through the foster care system. Was forced to become a stripper. Later I got involved with a kingpin. He took me out the clubs and put me in a nice situation and a home. We had a daughter. Things began to fall apart. Out of nowhere, he began to beat on me. Badly. He then moved on to be with someone else. This was after he tried to kill me! I took my daughter, and we got as far away from his ass as we could. I wanted to do better. I knew I could do better. So, I enrolled into the studies of the medical field. I made a lot of progress. We then relocated to DC, and I pursued a career. That's basically a snapshot synopsis of my life," Charlotte related.

She had a well-spoken way of how she blended lies with the truth. It sounded so believable, he had no choice but to accept all she'd said as authentic. Not to mention the fact that it came directly from her. Someone he already deemed an honest person.

I'm more than sure he'll never know my real truth, so why not give him a dose of them both? she pondered to herself.

"And your daughter's dad? Your ex?"

"Where is he? He's dead to us. Dude is so dead to me and my baby. Not relevant on any level! So please, I'd appreciate it if you not ask me about him. Okay?" Charlotte stated. "He's not worthy of discussing. And in return, I won't ask you about any of your exes or flings you once rotated. Deal? I don't want to know nothing about you before I came into your life. Absolutely nothing. That's why I've never asked. Now, do we have a deal or what?"

She now demanded his compliance.

Murder paused. He thought long and deep over her words. Finally, he replied, "I only wanna know one thing before I agree to your offer."

"And that is?"

"If any, what concerns do I have to worry over as it applies to you? Like, seriously?"

Charlotte now had to pause, so as to think of a dynamic response. She knew it was important to be reasonable. And, not to mislead.

"Truth be told, the only thing you'll have to concern yourself with is coming up with thoughtful ways to keep me interested in you and the program you put us on evolving. And having high status is the thing that makes me have an orgasm. Never forget that. Strength and discipline as a man to handle me, always help too. But no worries, not on my end. And I don't have any questions for you. I'm hoping the same will apply for me," Charlotte stated.

Murder had no reservations at that point. Charlotte was sure to place everything in context with her words.

"That's a deal. You got my agreement," he stated.

Charlotte produced a wicked looking smile at him. It appeared as if she was attempting to place him under a spell or something to the effect. She spoke once more.

"Good. Now come here. I'mma suck your dick for you tonight, because you've earned it. But I'm not gonna give you any pussy so fast. It's too soon," she teased with a smile. She knew the right words to use to arouse him into action.

Charlotte then gripped his manhood, pulled it through the slit of his boxers, stroked it twice, then went down on him. Dude was falling in love with everything about her. The quality time proved to be amazing.

The female formally known as "Carmen" knew exactly what trick to pull from her large bag of seductive ways. Any sexual advance always worked. No matter the time or the place. The level of control and dictation of sexual energy shall always rule the day. Also, any type of affair.

Fourteen

One Week Later . . .

Murder had an important meeting to attend. It was with a guy he deemed a mentor of some sort. A discussion was needed, being that Murder brought it to the elder city councilman's attention that he now had a female in his life to help keep him on the right track. Not to mention the fact that she'd moved him in the right way to do an act he'd never so much as thought of, let alone doing. And that was making a donation to a non-profit foundation. And a large amount at that. But the bottom line was, he felt really good about doing so. And had intentions to do so again, at the next opportunity. It was definitely a good thing for a street cat like him, who had known nothing but the low life and the gutter of society.

Murder was introduced to Major Appleton through the cop brother of his. This took place nearly two years before the day.

Councilman Appleton also acted as a sort of mentor to Jabari as well. Jabari wanted to be properly groomed and trained by Major, to someday have a run for a seat in the municipal building in Philly, once he'd put in enough years as a cop. He wanted his resume to really stand out by the time he was to begin a campaign, so as to convince voters he was the one.

The councilman owned a mansion in West Chester, just on the outskirts of the township. Although he was legitimate in civil society and paid his taxes, Major still had a hand in on the illegal pie the underworld produced. Many other powerful figureheads played the game as well. Some make it. Some don't.

Major knew some of everything that went on beneath the surface of the naked eye. And he also knew almost everybody who played a part. Played a part in the distribution and sale of narcotics throughout the city, from federal judges to the mayor, throughout the police department, all the way down to the head official of the sanitation department who had the duty to pick up trash. Councilman Appleton had connections to help advance him along the way. He utilized Murder to do his dirty deeds in the streets in exchange for helping him and Jabari at times when they needed him to.

Murder made it to Major's home. The time was just past 3:00 p.m. A Saturday afternoon. The councilman and his single man security personnel were the only two there. The wife and the teenage daughter were out on a shopping spree.

Murder was casually dressed. Major always liked to see the young street don presentable. Not looking like a fucking hoodlum who knew nothing but the ghetto. Major would often say to him, "If I'm in the business of doing business with you, you've got to always look like somebody, and act like somebody, if you want to continue to do business."

While seated in his car out front of the mansion, he texted to notify the councilman he was there. Murder was told to walk around the house to the backyard. The councilman was there on the spacious lawn. He was taking practice shots at a distance on glass bottles as the target. He'd not long before the day bought a couple of high-powered pellet air rifles and wanted to put them to work. Upon notice of Murder, he smiled, turned to take another shot, then turned back to give his guest the necessary attention the meeting required.

"Councilman Appleton!" Murder greeted. "How you doing?"

The two shook hands.

"I'm good, Barry," Major replied.

"I'm glad to have the opportunity to meet with you again to do business."

"Well, Barry . . . young brother. I'm glad to have you here at my place for us to negotiate business. If I didn't believe in you or didn't think you were capable to do things properly, we wouldn't have anything to talk about," said the forty-five-year-old municipal politician and distinguished African American gentleman. He was a slender guy, polite in manner.

Councilman Appleton stood at five foot eleven and weighed a hundred sixty-nine pounds. He was clean cut. Only a pencil thin mustache in facial hairs. His hair style was a low-cut fade. Major looked like an older version of another Philly native, Meek Mill. Only he had a lighter complexion of skin.

"So, what you had in mind to discuss, Councilman?" Murder asked. He was eager to get down to business.

The councilman exhaled in a disgusted way. "I've got some pretty interesting things developing in both high and low places. I'm trying to figure out which one may cause me the most harm if I don't quickly do away with them both first."

"Interesting developments in both high and low places you say, huh?" Murder retorted. "Business or personal?"

Major looked him sternly in the eyes. "Both," he then responded, handing Murder a pellet rifle at the same time to take a shot.

"If I had to choose between the two to deal with first, I'd say attack the one that's personal. Since business will always be business as usual. Much like politics," Murder offered his opinion.

"You make a good point. I thought on it in the same way. Just needed someone to confirm it for me."

"So, what you got in the way that troubles you? Or rather, who you got in the way?" Murder asked, then took a shot.

Ping!

He hit a target. The glass bottle shattered.

"An easy one to say the least. And then, one that may need more thought put into it. I don't want to ignite a drug war or cause any conflict where I work," Major stated. "I made a slight boo-boo, Barry. Something that's got to be cleaned up. I've got a potential rival who's looking to take my place. He sent a sleazy little bitch my way to seduce me. I fell for her moves and allowed the Jezebel to work one over on me. We went on a trip to Atlantic City one weekend. The problem is, she secretly recorded our date the majority of the time we were there."

"Damn! That's foul, ain't it?"

"That was the first time. But the worst part about it is, I slipped up and got the little slut pregnant. She, and my rival, threatened to expose things if I don't step down from my seat. Or if I don't pay her a certain amount by a specific time, once I do, relinquish my position as councilman."

"So, they're trying to extort you for your seat and your money?"

Major nodded his head in agreement to confirm what Murder asked.

"There's more."

"It is?"

"I've got those goddamn guineas down in South Philly so-called themselves trying to apply pressure at the docks of the port. They're also looking to extort some type of way. They causing a disturbance with our shipments of product."

"Ooh! Nasty ordeals on both ends. You definitely gotta do something to make these situations right," Murder remarked.

"Tell me about it!" Major let out, with a sense of anguish to his tone. "I've got a mess to clean up. And you, Barry, are the man I call upon to help me clean things up. Since the last two situations I had got resolved properly. On account of you," Major stated.

The councilman often had a bad habit of always speaking too formal at times. Typical behavior of a politician. He hardly ever comes to reality when talking to Murder, that he was a die-hard street nigga. Although he so happened to graduate high school at Benjamin Franklin High, he cared nothing about advanced formal education. Murder didn't give a fuck about being book smart or technical. However, he had plenty of street sense and common sense. And he was utilizing his smarts to put together a blueprint to an exit strategy out the game. At some point, at least. But when?

"Yeah, I hear you, Councilman. Loud and clear. And those last two pains in the ass of yours, I was sure to provide the prescription you ordered to do away with that pain, didn't I?"

"And I was sure to properly take care of you for your work, wasn't I?"

"No doubt. But let's cut the bullshit, Councilman. You and I both know that the more work I put in, the higher the price on the next. But it's not money I want this time around. I got a special request I wanna make on these two, since we already joined at the hip, anytime you got problems that need to be eliminated. If you know what I mean."

Pop!

Murder took another shot. He conveyed his message by letting off a round. The glass target exploded. This was the same way the head of the last victim terminated. A guy the Councilman wanted dead. Murder was the one to do the deed.

Major took a hard look at Murder. "You're finally beginning to see the bigger picture on this, huh Barry? That scares me in a way. I knew we would eventually get to this point. I just didn't know when."

"So, you never thought I was smart enough to realize how easy it could be for you to get rid of me and move on to the next man to replace me? It's business as usual," Murder declared in a serious tone.

"The same applies for you, with all you could use against me." The councilman felt the need to offer a reply.

"Yeah, well, I ain't no rat! And a blackmail almost always never goes good."

"And that's the reason why we're gonna continue to move like we have with doing good business. And whatever special request you got… I'm hoping I may be able to help you out with it?"

Murder didn't hesitate to make his request known. "You know what I want?"

"Please inform me."

"Once I take care of both these people for you, I want you to introduce me to the connect. The motherfucka' you getting the product from. That's not too much to ask, is it?"

The councilman eyed Murder sternly, raised his head, took a deep breath through his nose, and then responded, "So, you actually want me to give you the guy who supplies me?"

"No doubt, I do. I feel like I should be good enough for that, behind all these bodies I got piling up at your behest. To at least know who you know and pay what you pay for the product we're supplied. Our business should be mutual, since we together on this," Murder stated emphatically to his elder mentor.

"I tell you what. I can make that possible. I can simply put it to the supplier that you're my nephew and the one in line to run things on the streets, once I move farther into the political world. That's all there is to it," Major declared.

"I don't give a fuck what you tell him, so long as I know we got a deal. Do we, or don't we?"

"We've got a deal," the councilman declared as he turned to face his guest. They shook hands. A new deal was completed.

Murder now wanted specifics on the people Major wanted him to kill.

"Okay, so, the female. Is there any other way we can deal with her other than by death?" he asked. He definitely did not want to whack a pregnant chick. By no means.

"You got any better ideas for her?"

"I may do. Since it's on me to get both jobs done, ain't no room for error either."

"And once you take care of them both, the evidence they're trying to blackmail me with is going away with them. Then I can get back to being happy and stress free, doing what I do best, serving the public and being the people's champ," Councilman Appleton stated.

"Sounds like a solid plan. But here's the thing. In addition to me being allowed to meet the connect, I need to be paid extra too. Remember, the price goes up each time. I'm a contract hitter for you. And I deal dope to take care of me and my business. I do murder for hire. And I sell bricks of boy to make a profit. The price of life can be expensive. And the ticket for a kilo can be as well." Murder was sure to clearly speak his mind.

"So, I suppose now that the cat's out the bag on what I need you to do, I don't have any choice but to do all you want me to do, because I can't go to nobody else."

"Exactly, Councilman. You already know how this goes. It's without saying."

"I'm aware. But what else you asking for, to go along with wanting to meet the supplier at some point?"

"For two bodies. A dude and a pregnant chick. That's a hunnid grand, all day. Nothing short of," Murder stated. He had a lot of conviction to his tone. He didn't want Major to think for once he'd settle for less. Not one penny short.

"I need seventy-five up front. And once I take care of the job, I get the last of it. We clear on that?" Murder said.

"We are. We're good," Major responded. He then took a brief pause. He spoke out again. "One of my contacts will be in touch to pay you the money you ask. And until then, thank you for your time. And you have a blessed day."

"You do the same, Councilman. *Boom!*" Murder said, then made the sound of a gun being fired.

Murder then pulled his Glock-19 from his waistband. It had an infrared beam on it. He took aim into the trees of the foreground, then let off a shot.

Boom!

He hit a large hawk directly in the chest, killing it. The bird of prey was perched on a branch of a tree. The two men watched it tumble over other branches on the way to the ground. It was dead as shit. Much the same as the victims Murder had put in the dirt for the councilman.

Murder left the home, now on a mission to get rid of the problems Major Appleton had.

Fifteen

One Week Later . . .

The ambitious and aspiring Philadelphia municipal political figure, Errol Lawler, awakened from his sleep at his home at 3:00 a.m. like always for years. He would always stretch thoroughly, have a protein shake, then head to the basement for a jog on the treadmill. His wife and their two kids were upstairs still asleep. They didn't have any pets. Not cats to purr nor dogs to bark.

Errol's home was located in the Bella Vista section of the city. A nice well-to-do neighborhood to live, especially for African Americans such as Errol and family.

Errol had his head roving about inside the refrigerator, getting his hands on the orange juice container and fruit to go along with the shake he was intent on making. He hated milk. Although it had a good amount of protein itself.

He raised his body straight again, then closed the door to the fridge, causing the lighting to go dim once more. As he made a turn to go towards the island counter, there stood a ski-mask-wearing individual who was also cloaked in a black sweatsuit. He had a pistol with a silencer on it, trained directly on Errol.

"Not too loud, and not too many words," the armed assailant muttered.

"What the fuck!" Errol responded. "Who the fuck are you? What the fuck you want?"

"You ran afoul, Errol. You went too far. You did too much. And now, I've been hired to come pay you a little visit," the intruder stated.

"Who sent you?"

"Now, you know I can't tell you. Then I'll have to be paid to kill you twice," the intruder let out in response to the promising councilman. He still maintained a steady aim at Errol.

"So, somebody put you up to do a hit for him, I assume. Can we at least talk this over?"

"You should already know why I'm here. And there's nothing to be discussed between you and me. I got a contract to fulfill. In blood!" spat Murder, the masked man.

Tears began to flow down Errol's face. He trembled from fear, then pissed himself.

"Dude, you have any idea who I am? Or all I represent? You're making a terrible mistake, my brother. A terrible one, son."

"Let me be the judge of that. I don't get paid to compromise or work out plea agreements. My money comes when I take the life of somebody," Murder declared.

"Son. Listen to me, please. And listen to me well, okay? I'm an upstanding tax paying public—"

"You *was* all that!" Murder spat through gritted teeth. "But not anymore." He cut Errol's words short with the insult. The sharp remark stunned the once hopeful politician.

"Son, I have a wife and two kids up those stairs—"

His words got cut short again.

"And if you try to make a break for it, I'll just simply swap out your life for theirs," Murder sternly declared. He still had the pistol trained on the intended target. "To be honest, I'm really doing you a courtesy here, Errol, with all the chit-chat we doing. But I was told to at least hear your side of the story. Briefly."

"The side of what story you talking about? I'm curious to know. Because I've never done anything to have a gun pointed at me. Let alone, by someone having a choice to end my life or to let me live, resting at the tip of their finger. A trigger fingertip at that." Errol was honest with his words.

"There's a first time for everything, Errol. A last one too. Your first time having a gun pointed at you. And the last breath of air you take. So, we might as well go ahead and get it over with!" Murder spat.

"Alexa, call nine-one—"

Ptui!

Murder let off a round from his gun. He hit Errol square in the chest, causing him to stumble backwards onto the refrigerator, then collapse to the floor of the kitchen.

Ptui!

Another round spat, hitting him in the chest yet again.

Ptui!

Then a final round to the forehead to finish him off.

Half the problems that councilman Appleton faced was eliminated with the assassination of Errol Lawler, and whatever evidence he so-called was intent on using. It was now on to the next portion of the contract. One that may pose a moral threat to go along with it.

Sixteen

Charlotte found herself really taking a liking to the new boyfriend she had in her life now. She made it her business to relate to Imani the details of the date she and Murder went on. The deed Murder did was brought to her attention. Charlotte told her all about the dick sucking she put on Murder as well. The desire to settle down once more was a desire she held. The thought of marriage passed through her mind as well. A normal peaceful life as a mother and wife and a medical professional was what Charlotte truly wanted. And she was in the process of seeing to it the dream became a reality.

Imani was happy for her friend. And at the same time, she wanted to experience all over again the feeling and the appreciation which Charlotte now was grateful to have. Since her own marriage had already gone to hell in a perfectly wrapped gift basket.

Imani secretly envied Charlotte, in a good way. And wanted nothing but the best for her friend, believing that it was she who made the claim to Charlotte, that she thought Philly dudes were a better catch than the DC jokers. Charlotte thought the same herself. There was something about the aura, the attitude, and the mystique those Philly cats had given off at the party they attended, to cause both of them to think the way they did.

And although Imani didn't invite one of those dudes into her life that day as did Charlotte, she did have a particular guy in her sights. The one who was next to Murder all that evening. It was his right-hand man, Herb. She figured if he was as close to Murder physically as he was, Murder must keep him around a lot. And she now had a way to communicate her interest to him.

Imani was visiting Charlotte on this day. Her and her daughter. The four of them were looking to make it a girls' day out to get their hair, nails, and toes done. Ni'Asia and Farrah were in the back room enjoying themselves, while Charlotte and Imani were in her room having a conversation as Charlotte got dressed.

"Judging by the smile you've kept on your face and the high level of energy you've had, I take it you and the Philly guy, *Barry*, are heading in the right direction," Imani said to initiate talks in that area.

"Ooh... girl, yes. The right direction may be an understatement. We may be on the stairwell to heaven, boo. I'm so loving the way things are going," Charlotte responded.

"Well damn, girl! The sex that good?"

"You wanna know what's funny about that?"

"What, girl?"

"We haven't even had sex yet. As bad as I wanted it," Charlotte revealed.

"Get the heck outta here!"

"I'm for real, 'Mani. I'mma hold out for as long as I can. I want the buildup of anticipation to be epic," Charlotte declared.

"But why? If you feeling him and he feeling you, what you holding back for? I'm pretty sure he not trying to hold back on you. Or is he?" Imani asked with a smile.

"He's not. But I just know the type of power a female holds over a man by making him chase after the pussy and do whatever to get it. You get where I'm coming from on that?"

"Seriously, I do. But I haven't seen you this happy ever, throughout our entire friendship. The whole time we've been knowing one another, Charlotte. And I'm curious to know, why at work, Doctor Henderson all of a sudden seems to be so happy to see you now when she does? And you two have gotten all close and shit! Did I miss something, girl?"

Charlotte looked at Imani and smiled wildly. She then offered a response to everything Imani wanted to know, gaslighting in the process.

"Well, if you must know, darling, that was Doctor Henderson's dinner party Barry and I were invited to. She really liked the way we conducted and carried ourselves at the event. Not to mention, Barry was one of the top donors to her charity foundation that evening," Charlotte said.

"With me knowing what little I do about Doctor Henderson, I'm sure there were others there she felt the same about, especially with money like that to provide. It definitely has to be more to it than that. Besides, Doctor Henderson always got this look about her face, like you was responsible for saving her life or something. Like you and Barry have more of something she's aiming to get. Now, be for real with me, Charlotte." Imani pursed her lips, cocked her head to the side and demanded Charlotte to cut the bullshit.

"Money always has the power to change people and their attitude towards you and make them respect you more. Barry made a generous donation on our behalf to her charity foundation. It was for cancer research and other things," Charlotte revealed.

"I knew it had to be more to it. So, it wasn't so much of him making a donation, it was the amount of money he donated, right?"

"Right."

"So, not only is Barry a street dude with a gentleman side to him. He's got a *bougie* bone in his body too, huh?"

Charlotte turned to have a look in Imani's direction once more. She cooed and added a slight snicker to the remark Imani made.

"He has a lot of class about himself, 'Mani. He'll definitely fool you if you didn't know him."

"That was one hell of a donation, I see," Imani remarked.

"It was. He paid for our meals, which were a hundred and fifty each, to go along with the donation. It earned us an honorable mention that night. Me nor him have ever had our name spoken of so well. It felt so good inside. Every time I think about him now, I get these tingles racing up and down my spine. I love the feeling. No other man has ever made me feel this way. Not even my daughter's dad. Barry is turning out to be the answer to my wishes," Charlotte stated very confidently.

"Well, to me, he's definitely cut from a different cloth. Because most dudes don't even know how to spell romantic, even if you had them look it up in the dictionary. Let alone figure out how to be romantic anymore. And you're not lying to me, are you, girl? About you two not having sex yet?"

"No, 'Mani. I'm not lying to you. The only thing I did was give him a really good blow job. And that was only to keep him going. And not get the wrong impression like I'm the type of bitch who is playing hard to get. That's all. This kitty cat of mine throbbing though for that nice piece he's got situated between those fit legs of his."

Imani's mouth flew open. Her eyes lit up behind Charlotte's choice of words. She had a question for her.

"Well, is his friend anything like him?"

"His friend?" Charlotte retorted. "Which friend?" Her immediate thoughts went back to the day she and Shug hooked up with Reign Man and his home boy Breezy. It was déjà vu. The same scenario looking to repeat itself, years later.

"The guy who was standing to his right at the party. He had on this fly-ass Gucci velour sweatsuit."

"I'm aware of who you talking about. I'll be sure to let Barry know to tell his friend you checking for him."

"Please do. Maybe the four of us could do a double date sometime soon? Or attend another one of Barry's events together. If that sounds like something you could agree to?" Imani asked.

"We'll see. We'll see how it goes. But hey, we've got to get moving. Don't want all the nice stuff to be gone by the time we get there, now do we?" Charlotte let out. She then picked up her pace to get dressed.

The casual conversation between the two continued on as they discussed many topics.

PART THREE

Seventeen

Murder had a Puerto Rican female on the team who operated as a courier. She'd not long before the hour completed her rounds to the various heroin havens Murder and company owned, delivering packages and collecting money from the day's works. It was a Saturday night, and business turned out really good for the crew. Her name was Angela, aka Angie. Her duties required that once she drops off then collects, she'd go to her apartment (she lived alone) in Washington Square, call her capo (Herb) to stop by to pick up the money she had, and wait for him to show up. Sometimes, Herb would show the same night. And if not, first thing in the a.m., depending on what he had going on.

The time was 1:45 a.m. For the most part, the bars, clubs, and other night life party zones were on the verge of closing. There were tipsy patrons and others all about the Washington Square neighborhood, looking to get their freak on as they made their way to the next destination.

Angie entered the doorway of her apartment building. She had nearly ninety grand in tow, tucked away in the backpack she carried. The doors to the elevator opened. She stepped inside, looking to head up to the fourth floor. Before the doors closed, there appeared a Spanish couple. A male and a female, possibly Puerto Rican themselves. They'd just left the bar. The same one Angie made a stop at to grab a few beers to drink before falling sound asleep. It looked like it might be one of those nights Herb didn't show but would do so early the moment after sunrise.

The couple stopped the doors of the elevator halfway from closing and entered. To Angie, they looked like they were feeling really good. They were all smiles and smooching on one another heavily.

Not even five seconds inside the elevator, the female of the couple pulled a gun suddenly, and was aggressive in pressing the barrel of the pistol into Angie's chest.

"Bitch, gimme that fuckin' bag right now!" the female stick-up artist demanded.

The doors to the elevator were still open. The robber was looking to make a clean getaway. She so-called herself having good timing. There was no one else in the lobby, a clean slate between the elevator and the front door of the building.

"What are you doing?" the male of the couple let out. He had no idea what was taking place.

Apparently, the guy had recently met the female and was looking to have a good time with her sexually.

The female assailant turned her head to look at the guy, momentarily taking her eyes off of Angie. This turned out to be all the time Angie needed to make a move and react.

Angie swung sideways with her right hand aggressively, hitting the arm of the robber, knocking the pistol to the floor. Angie then reached inside her waistline and withdrew the gun she had. It was a .380. Angie cocked it and took aim. By the time she was able to do all that, the assailant had grabbed hold of her back-up too. a shiny, sharp 'Hawks-beak' nine-inch knife that was thin in structure and sturdy.

Swish!

The assailant got off a good downward swipe on Angie's face. The tip of the blade had no problem leaving an ugly result behind the effectiveness of how sharp it was. A nasty six-to-eight-inch gash opened on the left side of Angie's face. Her back hit the wall of the elevator. She slumped to the floor, holding her face with both hands.

Blood pulsated profusely down Angie's face onto her hands, clothes, and the surface of the elevator floor. The female assailant turned to run.

Pow!

Angie managed to get off a shot, even with blood in her eyes and her vision blurry. But she missed the female target and hit the dude instead. He was struck in the forehead as he stood and looked on at the fiery fighting. He slumped between the doors of the elevator, stopping them from closing. His eyes were wide open, although he was dead as ever.

In addition to the money Angie had, there was also a quarter of a kilo strapped to the small of her back. So, making a call to the cops to report the incident wasn't even an option. Even if she was on the verge of dying and another was actually dead.

The backpack Angie carried that had the money in it was snatched by the female attacker when the slashing was put upon her robbery victim. The only description Angie would be able to make to her capo and Murder of the assailant was that the female had on a pair of metallic royal blue Louboutin red bottom high-top sneakers. They had a silver tip on the toe area.

Angie then grabbed the dead guy by the ankles and dragged him inside the elevator to allow the doors to close. She then ripped the guy's t-shirt off him to use to apply pressure onto her face to control the bleeding. She reached her apartment floor, rushed to the door of her unit, went inside then texted an urgent message to her capo for him to hurry and get there. She'd been jacked, and also needed medical attention.

The crew Angie was a part of had a particular protocol in place that no matter what, always contact their capo first before anybody else. And the capo would decide what to do or who else to contact. If the situation isn't too drastic or too serious.

At no time could anyone be questioned by the cops. That could lead to problems on all ends. Even ones they didn't originally have. Angie followed the policy her leaders had in place. She was the first to put this particular one to use.

***

A fierce white female lawyer had been hired by a friend to represent her new client. A guy by the name of Jermaine Styles, better known on the streets as Black Jermaine. He was an inmate in the state prison system. The lawyer he now had filed a post-conviction appeal, an "Extraordinary Motion for New Trial." There were solid issues that could help him get free.

Jermaine was good friends with Murder and Herb. They all grew up in the North Philly neighborhood of Kensington. They used to hang out and hustle on the block together and also go to battle with other niggaz over street related issues. Of the three, Jermaine proved to be more hardcore and gangster, as he was a few years older and had taught the two younger bucks most of what they knew about street life. Back in those days, Murder wasn't really built like that yet. He wasn't truly trained to go. Therefore, the majority of street squabbles and predicaments of gun play were resolved by the ardent, brolic and fearless goon, Black Jermaine.

Jermaine was six-two, two hundred thirty-five pounds, and muscular. He was a former running back in high school. In appearance, dude would put you in the mind of the G-Unit commander and CEO, Curtis Jackson aka 50 Cent. They had the same physical features, and the same temp-fade Caesar hairstyle and beard trimming. Jermaine also had the swag and was suave as ever.

The issues which landed Jermaine in the pen to begin with were gun and drug possession. He had a Glock pistol, and fifty G-pack bundles he was looking to drop off at one of the trap spots his soldiers operated. The judge hit Jermaine with a sentence of fifteen to thirty to serve.

Although Jermaine didn't have to, he loved to be out on the block, knee deep in the action of the streets. He personally enjoyed getting his grind on and doing the work himself. A true general like he deemed himself to be. Dude was serious about that street shit, and ambitious too. Maybe a little too much of the two for Murder's comfort at the time.

Before the day Jermaine was arrested, he and Murder had connected with a new supplier. Murder was the one who found the plug, and so happened to put a plan in place to help advance the team. He held desires to be the leader of the crew at some point. That meant putting himself over Jermaine. Prior to this time, Jermaine began to aggressively take over and dictate to the others how he wanted things to go. A conflict was created between the agendas of the two. Something had to give to break the tension that existed. If not, it may have led to one killing the other. Murder killing Jermaine, or Jermaine killing Murder.

Jermaine was pulled over by the police while en route to deliver those fifty G-pack bundles. The reason for the police stop being executed, according to authorities, was due to a taillight on his new model Mercedes Benz S500 being out. The right side. So was the blinker light. Somehow, a tiny hole was drilled through the cover and penetrated both bulbs, disabling them from working.

Apparently, someone plotted against Jermaine and put to use one of their dirty tricks to have him moved out of the way. It had to be someone who knew his car and all he carried on his person. At least that night they did. Whoever put the cops onto Jermaine also knew he'd once been arrested for a firearm possession and a large quantity of narcotics with intent to distribute. If the same was to happen again, Jermaine stood to risk not seeing the light for a long time to come, hence the fifteen-to-thirty-year sentence he eventually was hit with.

Jermaine always held an attitude against the cops, especially the militant-type white cops who patrolled the neighborhood. To his misfortune, it was a militant white policeman who'd been tipped about Jermaine and pulled him over. A verbal altercation transpired between the two, compelling the cop to draw down on the street goon with his gun until back-up arrived. The car was searched, resulting in the gun and contraband discovery. However, through it all, there was a ray of light at the end of the dark tunnel Jermaine was trapped in.

An attorney-client meeting was granted to the lawyer and Jermaine. She made her way to Graterford State Prison to see him.

"Hello, Mister Styles. How are you, sir?" greeted Mrs. Eason. "It's a pleasure to meet you."

She was a pale-skinned, pudgy, middle-fifties white woman, with a short hairstyle that was pinned on both sides, exposing the studded set of earrings she wore. Her hair was white as fresh cotton, and her voice in tandem with her other features, made for one memorable character. She favored in many ways the looks of the former female chairperson of the Federal Reserve, Janet Yellen.

"It's a pleasure to meet you too," Jermaine responded. The two shook hands and then took their seats to begin things.

Jermaine continued. "I was told you'd be here soon to see me. If only you knew, how goddamn happy I am to see you!" he expressed in excitement.

"I was hired to do a post-appellate motions on your behalf. I've made some pretty interesting discoveries."

"Oh, you have?" Jermaine was now fully engaged.

"Absolutely, sir."

"Is it anything that's gonna help me get out the motherfucka' any faster?"

"There's a strong possibility," Mrs. Eason replied.

"How so? I'm dying to hear this shit." Jermaine was now totally interested in all the lawyer had to relate.

"Well . . . apparently, at the time of your arrest, there appears to be a set-up that led to it. There was someone who either called the cops on you, or was in cahoots with them to get you. The taillight on your vehicle was purposely disabled," the attorney made him aware. "At least, that's how I managed to read it upon my review of the record."

"You don't say. I knew something wasn't right about the whole situation. That was a brand-new Benz I had. It came straight off the showroom floor," Jermaine stated.

"You are correct about that, Mister Styles. I was made known of the fact from the VIN number of the car. The make, model, and year."

"Ain't no way a new whip like that—"

"A new whip!" Mrs. Eason retorted. "Excuse me!"

Mrs. Eason was obviously unaware of the slang term Jermaine used to describe the sharp new vehicle he once owned. He had to smile at her dumbfounded retort. He couldn't control himself from chuckling.

"But anyway, I'm aware somebody drilled tiny holes in my taillight to keep it from working. The streets are grimy as shit, Miss . . ."

She'd totally forgotten to provide Jermaine with her name.

"It's Miss Eason, sir," she stated.

"Miss Eason. Okay, gotcha."

"And it was that part, Mister Styles, that the prosecutor left out on purpose, as he would have had to explain the legality or lack thereof, on how the officer who executed the traffic stop, managed to leave the patrol district in South Philadelphia he was assigned to, then make his way to the north portion of the city, simply to locate your car and pull you over."

The attorney clearly explained to Jermaine the ace in the hole she had to help him get free after eight years inside.

"Damn! That cocksucker didn't even have any business being in North Philly no way, huh! I always wondered why I was transported to a South Philly precinct to be booked, and not one in North Philly," stated Jermaine.

"And therein lies your answer. The officer had no business away from his district to begin with. Absolutely none at all," Mrs. Eason confirmed. "I'm delighted to have the opportunity to be the first to tell you, Mister Styles. And that was also why the prosecutor never called upon the patrol officer to testify. He lied and made the claim that Policeman Horne was away on active duty in the military, when in fact, he was not."

"You're right. He never did show up at my trial," Jermaine remarked. "He was supposed to at least give his side of the story, then allow the chance for me and the lawyer I had at trial to challenge his testimony."

"And that's why I plan to argue Prosecutorial Misconduct and a Confrontational Clause Violation," Mrs. Eason stated. She laid out the legal terminology to explain bad behavior committed by the district attorney.

"Me personally, ma'am, I don't give a fuck what you call it! Just get me out the motherfucka', will you!" Jermaine let out with a smile. He could now taste his freedom. It was ever so close.

It was a female caller who directly contacted the precinct in South Philly that Officer Horne was assigned to. They did not dial 9-1-1. Officer Horne was definitely connected with someone in the underworld. But who? He'd been paid to pull over and arrest Jermaine. An absolute set-up for him to take a fall. The plot worked, and the person who wanted him gone was successful in doing so.

Eighteen

A Few Weeks Prior . . .

Before Mrs. Eason was hired to handle Jermaine's legal situation, he'd paid a proven "jailhouse lawyer" to go over his paperwork, to see if there were any errors, he could use to help get his convictions overturned. Indeed, the incarcerated paralegal discovered many technicalities throughout his review. Jermaine was sure to fact check what the guy brought to his attention in a phone call consultation with a third-party lawyer on the outside.

Throughout the time being served, Jermaine connected with a few dudes whom he was looking to build a team with once again. But it was this one particular cat by the name of Andre Holmes, aka Dre, who was from Philly himself, West Philly. Jermaine truly formed a bond with him. Dre served his time and was now free, after eight years inside.

Before Dre was arrested and locked away on drug charges, he ran a mediocre crew. Their products were crack-cocaine and powder cocaine. The team had certain territory in "the bottom" on 44th Street. Dre had everything in place to have a high level of success in the game again. The only problem was, he now needed to find a new connect to supply him. A lot had changed in those years he was gone, and a totally new way of doing business was necessary.

Nonetheless, Dre's mom still owned the small soul food café he bought for her before his arrest. She and her sister ran the joint. It once served as a hangout spot for him and the boys. And Dre's intentions were to do the same all over again. But this time, better. He now had a bona fide street veteran to back him and Jermaine. And it would also be Jermaine who would supply the crew with the new product (heroin) they were looking to deal with, once he completes the business of strong arming the supplier right from under someone he knew who had direct ties to the supplier themselves. Jermaine's contraband cell phone proved to be a powerful tool he put to use behind the wall, in a way like no other. He was extremely determined to be that "dark horse" whom no one saw emerging. His sheer thinking abilities and willpower put him on the path to taking the top spot.

However, he still needed Dre to continue in doing all he was doing and provide firsthand information on the politics of the streets and everything going on within the circles of both black and Spanish drug squads. Dre did so with ease. Also, he was the one who put up the bread to hire Mrs. Eason to represent Jermaine, his new big homie and mentor.

***

Murder was busy like crazy trying to get his record label, Murdoch Music Group, to pop and gain the exposure he so thought it was deserving of. He bought and renovated a building that used to be a haunt for teenagers. A party spot formerly called "Bobby Dances" located just off Broad Street and Girard Avenue. Murder converted the place to a pool hall on the lower level and a music studio on the second floor above it. He now spent a great deal of his time there, when not away on other business of his.

He got a call on his personal phone, the one which only family had the number to. It was Quana. She wanted to speak with him about someone. A person she was very close to, and so was he. The individual returned home to Philly after a brief stay down south in North Carolina with a boyfriend. The relationship fell apart and the two split.

"Yeah, what up, Quana! What it do!" Murder answered upon notice of her number on the screen of the phone.

He had his hat to the back, vibing heavily to the beat and lyrics of one of his young rising artists. Dude put some serious bars on display for Murder. He was trying to get an advance check. One Murder had no problem providing.

"What's good, bro!" Quana responded.

"Shit! Cooling. Here in the yo down at the pool room. One of my young *bouls* putting on for me. He spitting fire too!" What's on your mind? I hope you and whoever that boyfriend of yours is not having problems again, are you? Ain't no trouble in paradise, is it?" he asked with a touch of sarcasm.

"Nah, bro. Me and my dude in a decent space right now. I ain't gonna let any of those silly-ass jump-off jawns get between us no more. But anyways, I'm on my way to you now. I got somebody in the car with me who wanna see you," Quana said, then glanced over at that somebody she spoke of.

"Who?"

"You'll see when we get there, nigga! Have some patience. I promise, you gonna be happy to see them too," Quana stated.

"It ain't one of my used to be jump-offs, is it?"

"Nah, bro. You know I can't stand half them bitches no way."

"A'ight, I'm here."

"No doubt. We almost there now, headed down Broad Street."

"Check," Murder lastly stated.

The call ended.

Shortly thereafter, Quana and the female she had with her pulled up to the pool room on the narrow one-way street it was on. She parked directly in front, got out, and they both walked inside.

Murder's bodyguards had specific instructions to search any and everybody who wanted to go up the stairs and meet with him personally. However, them two niggaz dared not come at Quana like that. She didn't care what her brother told them to do. She wasn't having it. And was ready to spaz on Herb with a barrage of filthy, nasty, unforgiving curse words. He simply smiled and let the two pass without incident. He knew who the other female was with Quana. She was a close family member. A first cousin by the name of Tatiana, aka "Tati." Dude wasn't up for going through an argument with Quana. He had knowledge of her bipolar attitude.

The two female cousins stepped through the door to the studio. They greeted Murder.

"Oh shit! What up, Tati! How you been, girl?" Murder responded to the sight of their female cousin. He admired her a lot. The three of them used to hang tight growing up. They hustled together too. Heavy.

Murder stood to his feet and gave Tati a hug.

"What's good, Tati!" greeted Mondo. He was the rapper Murder had in the booth putting in work. Mondo was Murder's second cousin on his dad's side. No relation to Quana. However, Mondo did know who Tati was.

"What's up, Mondo. What it do, papi? I see you still at it, ain't you. I'm sure the rap thing gonna pay off for you both in a major way," Tati responded.

"How long you been back now, Tati?" Murder asked.

"A day or so now. You know I had to hook up with Quana, then eventually come holla at you."

They all took looks at one another and smiled brightly. The thoughts passed through their minds of all the fun they used to have coming up in life together. In the streets and otherwise.

"I know that's right. I'm sure you two 'bout to make some shit pop, for real-for real," Murder uttered.

127

He then had a thought. He could utilize Tati in a certain position for a particular purpose to help them accomplish something.

Tatiana was a pretty, bright-skinned dark hair having female. She was five-seven in height and weighed a hundred forty-one pounds, with a flat belly and had a wasp-like waistline. There was a slightly above average speedbump she had for an ass, with a nice set of headlights to match the other feminine qualities.

Tatiana's cute face and extraordinary features were out of this world, for her to be the daughter of a dope fiend heroin junkie she had for a father. He was Murder and Quana's uncle, Kevin, better known as Dollar Bill. Her mother was a Puerto Rican woman named Paloma. She got her beauty from her mother. Tati looked like the female recording artist Saweetie in many ways.

"What you got going for yourself, Tati?" asked Murder.

"Not a fuckin' thing, cuz! That's why I'm back home. Because I need to get back on my feet again. I allowed that bitch-ass nigga Teko, to take me down. but what the fuck do I know. When you love somebody, you love somebody. And you're blind to a lot of things. I'm aware now."

"So, you on your ass, basically?" Murder was blunt in asking. He was checking to know her financial situation.

"Ah, duh! Why the fuck you think I had to hurry to get in touch with you, nigga! I need you to put me on again. I'm tryna get situated in a place of my own again like I was before." Tatiana clearly made her intentions known to Murder.

Murder smiled and then shook his head from side to side at the witty straightforward reply Tati let out.

"You something else, Tati. You know that?" he remarked.

"Shit, I have to be honest with you, nigga. I'm a Fredricks. Dollar Bill Kev's one and only, playboy," she responded with more wit.

"You know what, I definitely got something in mind you can help me with. You two hold tight. And Tati, you come on. Let's take a ride for a little while. We need to talk about everything. Quana, you and Mondo chill until we come back. And I need to borrow your ride too. Okay?" Murder said to his sister and the rapper cousin. There was something important he really wanted to discuss with Tati.

Murder and Tati hopped in Quana's Beamer 5-Series. The inside of the car would provide the time and space necessary for him to lay out to Tati the very specifics of what he needed her to do. He had a nice payout for her once the job was complete.

Their tour took them to the North Philly neighborhood they grew up in. He made a pit stop at a local bodega. There was one particular person he needed to see and another he held a pretty good idea would most likely be at the store himself. He wanted snacks as well. A drink and a large bag of sunflower seeds. The ranch flavored ones. Dude loved those things. Tati wanted to refresh as well, so why not? She joined him in walking into the store. He needed to make a pick-up in the process.

Suddenly, lo and behold, Murder took notice of the one familiar face of the man he suspected would be somewhere in proximity. He was seated atop a stack of milk crates playing a game of chess with another guy. It was none other than his uncle, Dollar Bill Kev, Tatiana's dad.

"Daddy!" she yelped in excitement at the sight of him. Tati ran up to give him a tight hug.

Murder, on the other hand, wanted to see Kev but didn't want to. But he knew the importance of family and figured Tati would at least want to see her pop, no matter what his status or state of condition was. This was also one of the main reasons Murder went to the store to begin with. For father and daughter to connect. And for the other part he was in the process of putting into play.

"Hey, baby!" Dollar Bill responded. He was a frail man. He had on dingy, dirty clothes and a lint-littered wave cap. "Come here and give Daddy a hug," he said, then sat down the cigarette he was smoking on and stood to his feet.

Tati rushed to her dad, then coiled her arms around him tightly. She then planted a kiss on his recently clean-shaven cheekbone.

"How you been doing, Daddy?"

"I been good. I can use a helping hand though," he let out, turning his head in the direction of Murder. "Nephew, won't you throw a po' dog a bone or something!"

Murder offered no reply, only a cold stare.

Tati was so happy to see her daddy. The two had not shared a moment in quite a long time. Months to be exact. She'd been away down in North Carolina.

She held a long smile then hugged him tightly again. No matter how clean she was or how exotic she looked and smelled in comparison to how dirty, toxic and terrible he was, Tati didn't have any hesitations about embracing her father, kissing him, and showing love. Even with those signature pair of busted worn-out and worthless penny loafers he had on his feet being an embarrassment, she absolutely loved him. To the death.

Dollar Bill continued to look at his nephew. "What up, Barry! How you been?" he said to him, then tried to give Murder dap.

"Fuck you want, nigga!" Murder angrily spat. He hated his uncle.

"Be nice, Barry. Please," Tati asked of Murder. She needed him to calm down and treat her father a little better. At least that day. In the moment.

"Goddamn, nephew! It's still like that, baby?" Dollar Bill let out.

"Fuck yeah, nigga! It's gonna always be this way between you and me! Period! Ain't nothing else to be debated about that."

The two had never seen eye-to-eye. Their relationship had been sour for years. Similar to the situation between "Money Making Mitch" and his uncle "Ice" in the movie *Paid in Full*. "Well, I-be-damned! I wonder how my twin sister Karen would feel if she knew her son—my one and only nephew—treated me so fucked up the way he does? I am sure she's asked about me by now."

He caused Murder to reflect over how fucked up the personal grudge was he held on him. There still appeared to be no end in sight to it.

As for Dollar Bill, his choice of words for his nephew and proper English put on display, although he was a notorious junkie from hell and took pleasure in the life he now lived. He still possessed a high level of education and intelligence, as he graduated high school in the top one percent of his class and earned a scholarship to Yale University to major in business and account management. He "so happened" to have his beginning as a dope head and getting high while there. He dropped out as a freshman. The rest, as they would say, is history.

Dollar Bill's words triggered something in Murder's mind. A promise he'd made to someone.

"Fuck!" he muttered. It was important that he keep his word to this one particular person at least.

He pulled his phone from the clip of his belt. It was the latest iPhone. He unlocked only one app from the security feature. He then hit the icon button to begin a video call on *Messenger*. He continued to talk shit to his uncle as the call was going through. Someone on the other end finally answered.

"Here, nigga!" he barked, passing Dollar Bill the phone. "And the only reason I'm doing this shit is because I made Mom a promise that I would! So, consider yourself lucky, ol' nut-ass nigga!" he let out more.

Tati looked on at both of them, smiled, and shook her head at the same time.

Murder's mother, Karen was on the phone. She'd been dying to talk to her twin brother, Dollar Bill.

"And you better not take too long either, nigga! I gotta step to the back for a minute anyway," he said to Dollar Bill. "Hi, Mom! I love you!" he took a look into the camera and said to his mother. Murder then stepped off to the back of the bodega to handle business with the owner.

Tati remained put with her father and talked with her aunt.

Nearly five minutes passed. Murder now returned to the front area of the store. He took notice of his uncle and cousin smiling, laughing, and having a good ol' time in conversation with his mother. The boy couldn't help but to feel good inside and rejoice at the sight of his family, happy to be in contact.

"Okay, Karen. I love you and I gotta go. Here comes that mean-ass son of yours. Dolla Bill gotta go, baby girl. I'mma be sure to keep in touch too. All right? And when you say you coming home to visit again? I must've missed that part?" he asked his twin.

Karen responded by telling him, "Soon."

"Okay, I'mma be expecting you too. And I'll be sure to buy a phone sometime or another to call you more often. I'mma do that while I'm in the store now. But your son gotta break me off a few ends to get by with."

"Okay, nigga! Time's up! Gimme my goddamn phone," Murder let out with a smile this time. He wasn't so harsh now.

Murder exchanged a few more words with his mother before ending the call. She gave him an order on something she wanted him to do. He hated it but had no choice but to do what his mother said do.

He then pulled out a roll of cash and peeled off three hundred-dollar bills.

"Mom told me to be sure to look out for your bum ass, nigga! But didn't say how much. So here!" Murder declared, then gave him the money. "I'm sure the dope man about to get all that, so if you tryna get hooked up, you already know my man there got what you looking for. Get with him."

Murder actually had the audacity to insult his uncle, and at the same time, offer a suggestion to him on where he could go to buy the next fix he may be looking for. Like a heroin junkie didn't have any idea on where to locate the best dope to pump into their veins.

"First and foremost, thank you, nephew. I appreciate this. Lawd knows I do. But on the other thing, I'mma have to respectfully decline your offer. Because I've been trying to tell you for the longest. You selling the right product, but the wrong brand! That 'Black Tar' shit you dealing out of Mexico is good, but that other shit is great! Just like 'Tony The Tiger' said it. That's that goddamn 'China White' shit out of Asia I'm talking 'bout. And as a matter of fact, my black ass about to take two of these big-headed blue bills here," he held up the money and fanned himself with it, "go over to the spot where they pushing that great shit, and load my goddamn veins with a fix of that 'Eastern Venom' and pray I don't die! They got some shit floating round now that'll knock you on your ass as soon as you load up. And your uncle Dollar Bill gotta have it! I gotta be sure to buy a phone too, so I can keep in touch with your momma," he stated emphatically with all he related.

Dollar Bill had no shame in his game in speaking the way he had about his terrible addiction to heroin. His daughter simply looked on at him with a smirk on her face and slowly shook her head. She knew her dad was hellbent on getting high.

"A'ight-a'ight, nigga. Whatever. Don't kill yourself. Because more than likely, I'm gonna be the one who's got to pay for your funeral. So be easy, chump!" Murder lastly spat, adding humor to his remark. He caused the uncle to chuckle himself at the wise crack.

"Bye, Daddy. Here is my number, okay?" Tati said and passed Dollar Bill a piece of paper she'd written on. She then gave him a hug again, pecked him on the jowl, then began to follow Murder out the store.

"I love you, Daddy," Tati turned briefly to say.

Nineteen

Dee Dubbs, one of the crew leaders who worked for his brother G-Code, a dude who was cool with Murder, met up with him to have a brief discussion on the incident that happened with Angie, and the possibility the hit could be a coordinated one. An attack he and his crew were capo over, needed to possibly prepare for. The protocol was followed properly by Angie and Herb. And she managed to get the additional drugs off her person before being taken to the hospital to be treated. She was forced into the fate of having to go on about her life with the ugly permanent scar. However, she did walk away with her life. And that was enough for her to settle on.

The cops were called by hospital authorities and arrived to question Angie, the victim. Her story remained the same, that "she left a bar en route to a train stop, and some guy attempted to rape her. She fought him off but was cut in the process." A necessary lie that had to be told to prevent the truth from coming out. Besides, Angie was then taken across the bridge to New Jersey to the hospital because Philly PD had recovered a dead man at the apartment building where she lived. Good thing the lease wasn't in her name.

Murder and Dee Dubbs began to brainstorm over everything and try to figure out who may have taken aim at them. G-Code was out of town. They now knew the hit was a designated one, because there were two other distros in the network hit in a similar way. By a mid-height, fit female, with strong features. Spanish. And wore a pair of metallic royal blue, red bottom high top sneakers. Ones with a silver tip over the toe area. Angie also described her attacker in this way. The additional two who was hit, were Spanish. One survived. One died. They needed to track down this elusive hitter with a knife and put an end to their reign of terror.

***

The heroin supply in Philly began to dry up. There existed too many complications on all ends. The Italians basically began to dictate how things were to go at the Port of Philadelphia. Street crews beefed and waged battle over turf. They stepped on the toes of one another. The pettiness appeared to have no end.

The main heroin supplier—a Mexican national by the name of Gustavo Ruiz—found himself totally unhappy with the situation going on in Philly. He was made aware of the hitter on the loose there, that was doing heavy damage to people. A female at that. Leaving no trace or links to help identify who they actually were. Nor who could've possibly sent them.

Ruiz perceived that it became a "dog-eat-dog" scenario playing out and ordered his number one Philly distro, Councilman Major Appleton to get with his number-two guy, Chandler Rozier aka "C-Ro," and they both figure out what the problems are and resolve them. And until they did, he was putting a hold on distributing any product. And all they had left needed to be sold and his money paid.

Whether Major and C-Ro knew it or not, Ruiz was looking to force them out the way and replace them with someone he already had an eye on. He was a Spanish cat himself. The leader of the "LDN's" (Latin Dragon Nation.) Ruiz had only met those three out of Philly, no one else. The third distro's name was Felipe Valdez, aka "Highway."

C-Ro took the initiative to call a meeting of all the distros whom he, Major and Highway supplied. It was necessary to discuss business and do all possible to eliminate problems.

Most notably, find that fucking hitter and send that bitch to see her mother!

The meeting was scheduled for 11:00 a.m. two days into the future. The location chosen was an upscale Chinese restaurant C-Ro was familiar with. However, everything was subject to change at any moment's notice. Major was the one calling the shots behind the scenes. He couldn't ever be personally seen present on any meeting of that nature, due to him being a publicly elected councilman of the city, and the potential collateral damage which could befall upon him if caught on surveillance. And it would always be C-Ro to be the one to speak on behalf of Major. They needed to get shit together.

***

It was Major being the one to send out the group text to the others about the meeting, and where they would come together. He felt the sting of disappointment Ruiz held of him and wanted to get back in good grace with him at all costs. Rectifying the situation would serve the purpose. And especially so with the issues he had Murder correcting for him. Things had to be right between Major and Ruiz, being Major agreed to introduce Murder to Ruiz once both killings were carried out.

The three top distros who were directly connected with Ruiz were Major, C-Ro, and Highway each had a right-hand man under them. That was Murder to Major, G-Code to C-Ro, and the overweight leader of the Latin King Nation of Philly (LKNP) Gourdo to Highway. Each side wanted to look the others in the eyes, gauge their energy, and discern whether or not the hits taking place came from within the circle. They had questions. Hard ones. But at the end of the day, everyone wanted to iron out the differences that complicated business, get the supply line rolling again, and progress forward.

Murder and his two guys, Herb and Traino, came together to talk and brainstorm over all the situations they'd been forced to do battle with. To also try to pinpoint which of the distros had the most to benefit by having the others hit. Murder needed Herb and Traino to help him think. They also wanted to discuss Angie.

"Yo man, I been watching all them motherfuckas' closely, and I still can't seem to figure out who it might be," Murder initiated. "I've got a hunch though, it was somebody inside the circle of distros."

"To me, a good place to keep focus on is the crew who haven't gotten hit," Herb stated in response.

"Yeah, that do make sense. I don't think nary one of them motherfuckas' dumb enough to rob and hit their own people who work for them. And besides, of the four who got got, how important of a piece are they?" Traino asked of Murder.

His question captivated Murder. It was deep and insightful. Murder jarred his head. He looked on at Traino and offered his full attention.

"You got a strong point there, Traino. Now that I think about it, every last one of the people who got hit, played an important part of the crew they belong to. So, how the fuck would they know how important the particular person was, or the role they played? For instance, our Angie, being the one to drop off product and pick up money?" Murder stated.

"Okay, so let's narrow it down a bit to get the truth out of it. Of all the distros, whose crew got hit, whose crew didn't?" asked Herb.

"Shit, you got the nigga G-Code, who didn't get hit. You got that fat, sour ass motherfucka Gourdo, who didn't get hit. And now that I think about it again, that nigga C-Ro—the one who close to the guy I get our product from—he nor his crew didn't get hit," Murder made them aware. He now began to think.

What the fuck! Maybe that nigga Major the one behind all this shit! He probably trying to do something to keep me under his foot. Now that he has something on me for hitting the guy Errol for him, he could use it against me. And he might be trying to do anything possible to move me out the way to keep me from meeting the connect, he further contemplated.

"Murder, who exactly knows about the main plug? And who's met the plug directly?" Herb asked a very important line of questions. "Reason I ask, is because it's always some grimy cutthroat shit going on when more than one person knows about the connect," he added to give deeper thought about what the motive probably was.

"Bingo! You right, Herb. Ain't but two people who's done that. They know the plug and have met him. To my knowledge. And out the blue, one of them so happened to call me up and wanted me to meet at his place about some business he needed me to take care of. Unrelated to product. The deal was, once I get done getting busy for him, he would introduce me to the plug. In addition to other things," Murder stated. "And not only that, the motherfucka' mentioned that he and the other cat, who's actually met the plug before, the three of them met up again. This was before he had me to meet him. And not only that. He brought it to my attention that the nigga G-Code hit him up and wanted to negotiate a few things," Murder further said. He was careful not to reveal the name of who he was referring to.

"So, you mean to tell me, what we got going on here is the connect had a secret meeting with the top distro and the second in line, and the second in line so happens to be one of the distros whose crew didn't get hit? Is that what we dealing with now?" Traino asked. He put things into perspective.

"From the looks and sound of everything...yeah. That's what we dealing with right now. The crazy part to that is, we don't even know who's behind it. To at least hit back. We ain't got a target to focus in on," Murder uttered. He made sense on the reality of it all.

"The hell if we don't!" Herb spat. "To me, it's either the top distro in cahoots with the plug themselves—to get somebody out the way—or the plug who you deal with is in cahoots with one of the other distros in the network and looking to move them up the food chain behind the attacks. That's my take," Herb concluded.

"Nah-nah-nah. I don't think it's the guy I'm dealing with. Trust me, we got too much going on at the moment for it to be him. Me and dude too deep in business," Murder responded.

"Well, you did say y'all had a deal in place to where you're supposed to meet the main connect, right?" Herb asked. He was looking to make a point.

"No doubt. But like I said, we're in too deep in another area. He basically can't do away with me on some cutthroat, stab in the back shit. He needs me," Murder made it clear.

"And I understand that part. But that's not to say he can't make it hard for you on your end. You and others who depend on him for product. It's simple to understand, Murder. All they have to do is create chaos, make everybody go into a panic to where nobody selling anything, because they'll be too busy pointing fingers at each other. trying to figure out what's really going on. That'll leave everyone totally forgetting about what the ultimate goal is at the end of the day. And that is, product got to be supplied. Products got to be sold. Money has got to be made. And the main has got to get paid. The only way I can't see it no other ways is if the top distro, who is closest to the connect, had gotten hit too." Herb laid out a solid argument to force Murder to reason deeper.

"To be honest with you two, the supply line took a hit too, but that was because of something else out of the control of the top distro. The man who I deal with," Murder stated.

"You wanna help us understand that?" Herb let out.

"I can't speak on that. It was something me and the top distro had a private conversation about," Murder responded.

Herb was slightly offended by Murder's remark. "So, in other words, you mean to tell me, you got your two top guys here with you—me and Traino—who you trust with your money and your life, and who you depend on to help you get down to the bottom of all the bullshit, but you don't trust us enough to fill us in on everything going on with you? What part of the game is this, bro?"

"Come on, Herb. It ain't even like that. The shit just bigger than me, bro. But, if you must know, them motherfuckin' Italians causing problems over at the port," Murder informed.

"I got word of that from my gun guy Vladmir, of the same thing. He mentioned he and his Russian people been beefin' with the Italians for the past few weeks now at the port. I went to him to find out what new he had for sale. That's when he told me his people's container got robbed by the Italians. They had guns and ammo coming in, and luxury vehicles and expensive smart TV's going out. Vlad says the Marconi Clan are the ones behind everything. So, to retaliate, Vlad's people went out and robbed the warehouses where the Italians had their heroin and meth supply situated. They ended up killing one of the Italian watchmen in the process. All movement came to a stop. At least until the conflict is over with," Herb stated.

"I get it now. And that explains what the beef is all about at the ports. I didn't know before you just brought it to my attention, the Italians applying pressure. And now that I look at it, I believe that's what the connect has done. Like the Russians. Shut everything down until the bullets stop flying and the bodies not dropping any longer," stated Murder.

"Murder, to be honest, bro, I don't think we can continue to go on too much longer without being resupplied. Our people who move the work are getting antsy and won't be too happy to hear us telling them ain't no work at the moment. We need to tap into the reserve stash we sitting on," Herb said. "And I understand the logic of what the connect got going on. But bro, we can't continue to sit back and let the product we got collect dust. We need to move that shit," Herb stated emphatically.

"You definitely right about that, Herb," Traino chimed in once more to say. "We don't need a civil war poppin' off with our own people all because the three of us wanna go on strike. Motherfuckas' ain't gonna be happy if motherfuckas' ain't eating! I know the feeling all too well."

Traino seemed to be in agreement with the second-in-command on the matter. A vote was taken. The majority ruled the day. Murder was able to see things in the way Herb and Traino presented it to him.

The three continued on to discuss other matters that the team was plagued with. Herb proceeded.

"We still got Angie grumbling like crazy too, bro," he made Murder aware.

"Oh, word!" Murder retorted.

"Fuck yeah! Bitch complaining to me, talking 'bout her boyfriend done left because she's too ugly now with that scar. We had to shut her down from working because she'd be too easy to identify if any witnesses seen what all took place. And for some reason, Philly PD showed up at her door looking to question her behind receiving an anonymous tip from a female caller."

The actual hitter themselves, providing reports they saw a guy get shot in the head by a female who was cut in the face. And for the cops to get the surveillance footage of the elevator and the apartment building lobby. They would then know what all took place."

Herb related each and every word Angie said to him.

"What the fuck!" Murder let out.

"I know, right! Now the problems seem to wanna begin behind her," Herb retorted.

"Angie wasn't home when those cops came by, was she?" Murder asked.

"Nah, she wasn't. Thank God for that. Her sister was though. That's how we got the message. But if it was up to me at this point, I say we go ahead and clip the bitch, bro. That'll put an end to it all. No more questions by the cops. No more us being paranoid and worrying about the bitch flipping and ratting on us no more. None of that shit, bro! Period!" Herb spat his true take.

"Nah, bro. I don't think that'll be a wise idea. What type of message would that send about us, man? To the other crews who know about us being hit, and now looking on to see how we intend to deal with the situation? We can't do her like that," Murder responded to the suggestion Herb made.

"Again, if we go ahead and waste the bitch, we no longer have a situation to concern ourselves with. Now, will we?" Herb remarked sternly.

"Herb, listen to yourself, bro. If we actually do what you implying should be done, there'll be nobody else on the team who would want anything more to do with us. And would jump sides in a heartbeat," Murder stated.

"Not if we dress it up to make it look like we sent her out of town to now live," Herb let out.

"For what? To be buried? Everybody on the team already know how we get down, bro. And again, that won't be a good look on us. Angie is a loyal worker. One who followed protocol. To the letter. Did everything exactly how we told her to and said nothing to the cops. It can't get anymore real than that," Murder said emphatically.

"Yeah, that may be so, until the realness of her reality begins to set in! When she wake up one morning, go to the bathroom, take a look in the mirror, and finally come to terms that that once beautiful face of hers is now a horrible fuck! And her life is ruined forever. The bitch gonna immediately run to the cops at that point and throw up all she knows about us. I'm just telling you, bro, she's collateral damage, Murder. She just is," Herb gave his thoughts once more.

"I hear what you're saying, bro. but I tend to think differently about Angie because of how well I know her," Murder responded.

Herb rolled his eyes and shrugged his shoulders behind Murder's remark. "Hey, it's your call, bro. It's on you on what to do next. Just don't say I ain't warn you when shit hit the fan. A'ight?"

"Well, at least we do agree on something out the situation. That it is my call to make. That I call the shots and my decision is to let her live. To live long enough to see another day, no matter how ugly she may look now. And while we at it, take her a bouquet of flowers for me, give her twenty grand, a greeting card, and send my regards. This should be an end to the issue, I would imagine," Murder lastly stated on the Angie ordeal.

"No doubt, bro. If that's what you want me to do," Herb replied.

Traino nodded his head to agree to the peaceful resolution brought about between them.

"Now, back to this upcoming meeting between all the distros. I can't wait to have the opportunity to look that nigga G-Code in the eyes and see what type of lie he's gonna come up with, to take the heat away from him as being the motherfucka' who's hittin' everybody!" Murder spat vehemently.

Their long in-depth conversation continued.

***

Three Hours Later . . .

Following the long strategy meeting Murder held with his two guys, he made his way to Center City, Philadelphia. He owned a two-bedroom, two-bath, sixteen-hundred-square-foot penthouse suite there. The posh living space was located at The Muran Condominium Building at 2101 Market Street, near the heart of the city. Murder paid a grip in rent every ninety days for two years until the place was fully paid off.

And, of all the locations he owned, he loved the penthouse the most. He felt safer there and more complete as a businessman anytime he stood at the window of his 40th floor suite and looked at the city from high up. Dude was obsessed with the thought and the feeling experienced of being one of the fortunate ones, way up high, looking down at others and the ground level beneath. He was power struck and infatuated with gaining more.

Oftentimes, Murder allowed a young girlfriend of his to live in the penthouse and have her way. He'd known her and had dealings well before Charlotte came along. Her name was Brooklyn Carter. She was a sexy, slim-figured, dark-skinned cutie. Someone Murder had in his life on and off the past five years.

Originally, Brooklyn hailed from none other than New York City. The Borough of Brooklyn, to be exact. She arrived in Philly to attend college at the University of Pennsylvania. She was eighteen at the time when the two met. Brooklyn acquired a master's degree in business and account management. She was one of his trusted people to handle all things financial for the kingpin boyfriend.

Brooklyn's time was split between New York City and Philly. And for the most part, her stationary position was there in her hometown community with family. She and Murder had a strange relationship. Nonetheless, it was a working one. Anytime they spent quality time together, the feelings they shared were intense, but lately, a wedge was now situated between them. One named Charlotte. He knew how to balance his time between the two.

Murder was at the penthouse this evening brainstorming, thinking intensely over everything, eager to put a finger directly on who the guilty person was behind the hits. The evidence pointed at two potentials, G-Code or Gourdo, being that neither of the two were targeted and stood to benefit the most within the network, if in fact, they moved up the food chain.

Throughout his contemplation, a familiar someone came to mind. A person he knew that if no one else had any information on all that was going on in the streets, this one particular dude did, despite the restricted situation he found himself in, and Murder being the potential person who put him there. It was Black Jermaine.

Through it all, the dude Jermaine managed to keep his ear pinned to the ground and was tuned in on every beat from the pulse of the streets. Besides, it was he who taught Murder the majority of all the street shit he was learned in, as they previously ripped and ran the streets of North Philly (the Bad Lands), before Murder's plan was executed to the max, to put him over the top.

Jermaine made serious strategic moves from a contraband cellphone he had in prison. It was like he was still on the turf out and about, and not locked away as he were. And all the networking he was doing had the potential to thoroughly work out in his favor, being that his newly hired lawyer Mrs. Eason, found major legal flaws with his case. Ones that would help him get free sooner, rather than later.

Murder had recently gotten word from an associate of his that Jermaine wanted him to call. They needed to talk. It had been a long time since they'd done so. A number was provided. Murder made the contact. He texted first to make Jermaine aware it was him.

MURDER: *Yo! DSJ! What's good. It's me. Redrum. This you, right? Hit me up.*

Shortly thereafter, Jermaine replied.

DSJ: *Yeah, nigga! Lol! This me. Call now.*

Murder then made the connection.

"Pop your shit, nigga!" Jermaine answered in his signature gangster idiom.

Both of them had to chuckle at his words. Jermaine hadn't changed much at all.

"Motherfuckin' dark-skinned Jermaine! My nigga! What's been good, dawg! Long time," Murder responded.

"Damn right it has. But I'm still alive, nigga. What you got going?" Jermaine declared.

"Same shit, different day, but a better way," Murder stated.

"I know that's right. And word is, you doing good out there, nigga. You wanna share some of the good news with me? They say you living lovely. That you having your way out there. Catch me up to speed, homie."

"That commissary money you get every month increased, didn't it?"

"No doubt."

"A'ight then. That's catchin' you up to speed and giving you the good news all at once," Murder declared. "But on the flipside to that, I've got a few issues I may need you to help me figure out."

Jermaine had already been thoroughly informed by Dre of the magnitude of the drama playing out on the streets. He simply needed Murder to fill in the blanks.

"Oh, yeah! You do get that part done. No doubt about that. The dough has been proper. But back to you, what you got on your mind you trying to figure out?" Jermaine asked.

Murder delved right into the details of it all. He mentioned names, times, dates and past incidents to Jermaine, doing essentially what he needed him to do, fill in the blanks.

There clearly was a high degree of trust between the two as Murder valued the insight and reasoning of mind Jermaine had, as Jermaine's advice always seemed to prove the advancement of Murder's cause.

There was a lot related by Murder. Probably more than what should have been related. And he felt no need to worry, as Jermaine had never shown any forms of treachery.

However, the golden rule always reigned supreme. To "Trust No Man," "Trust No Bitch!" Nor to trust anyone based on the past. Period!

Jermaine responded to what was asked of him. "But yeah, no doubt, Murder. I'mma check into a few things for you then get back to you in a few hours. You gonna be up, right?"

It was a Wednesday night, 9:00 p.m.

"For sure, bro. I'mma be right here, chilling in my penthouse suite. I've got a few other calls to make and some other business to attend to as well," Murder responded as he now entered the master bedroom of the condo from the living room area, took a glance at Brooklyn's naked body, and became instantly aroused.

She'd just gotten out the shower and was now applying moisturizing cream to the silky-smooth skin of hers.

The call between Murder and Jermaine came to an end. He then sat his phone on the nightstand next to the bed. Murder placed his hands on his hips and simply looked on at Brooklyn doing all she was up to. His observation of her was like she was performing an exclusive exhibition ballerina art show. It was beautiful to witness.

Brooklyn rotated her head to the left, locking eyes with him. She had one leg atop the bed and the other planted on the floor, graciously massaging the pleasant-smelling cream onto one leg at a time.

"So, you gonna just stand there and look? Or are you finally gonna attend to this here? It's been a minute," Brooklyn teased, with her sensational sultry voice. "I've been on hold long enough." Her vocabulary and speech were proper. Evidence of her cultivated background.

"Oh, I'm definitely in the mood to attend to that there tonight, sweetie," Murder responded to her pleasing invite.

At that point, he then began to strip down out of his clothes to his birthday suit. The same as Brooklyn had on display.

Murder then walked over to her. They stood face-to-face. He wrapped his arms around her slim waist, making those C-cup chocolate breasts of hers firmly plant on his chest. Their eyes locked and they began to tongue kiss in a slow and passionate way.

Brooklyn eased the palms of her hands down the wings of his tight back, over his fit waistline and lastly, resting on those hardened ass cheeks of his. She was obsessed with how his butt muscles felt in the space of her hands. She squeezed him then strode her palms over his rock-solid thighs. Murder was a bit of a fitness nut. He had one hell of a physique and was in good shape.

"Brooklyn! Tell me exactly, how do you want this dick tonight?" He gave her the option to choose her pleasure.

The response she gave clearly let him know the particular mood she was in.

"Barry! I-don't-give-a-fuck how you give it to me. So long as I get it! Okay! I need it in my life," Brooklyn let out in a purring-like fashion. She was definitely eager to be fucked.

No thought of Charlotte crossed his mind for this occasion. It was all Brooklyn. The whole time.

"No problem, baby. You can have it however you like. Now turn that ass of yours around!" he demanded. "I'm about to fuck you hard and fast from the back. Only rough sex tonight. We can do that lovemaking shit some other time," he capped off his remark.

Brooklyn began to rotate her body. "Ooh! I love it when that street shit from you meets that smart shit I've got to offer. A perfect culmination," she cooed playful banter.

She then continued to stand at the foot of the bed. He had the best viewpoint of all the world for any man to have. Brooklyn's whole backside and beautifully exposed private area was indeed a masterpiece of creation from the Most High above. Couple that with his high-rise lofty view which overlooks the Philadelphia City skyline, and you have a double delight of sublime scenery.

Brooklyn's love cave down below was clean shaven, had a fresh pink texture of color down the credit-card-like slit, puffy, and permeated an aroma which wars of the world would have fought over. The nostrils of Murder were invaded like DEA agents would raid the busiest drug house in all America.

Whop!

He smacked her on the ass hard.

"Ooh!" Brooklyn cooed. She then arched her back deeply, now dying to be penetrated.

Murder was piped up and ready to get to it. He eased in closer with the seven-inch manhood of his, situating the head at the entry point of her gate to heaven. Dude then lulled a large amount of drool from his tongue onto his dick and swiped the head up and down her slippery slit. He penetrated, gliding inside smoothly.

"Ahhh!" Brooklyn let out in exhale. She had an orgasm then and there in the moment, coating his dick with the cream of her release.

Brooklyn must've really been backed up for her to get one off that fast. Nonetheless, she had plenty left to relieve herself of. Her reserve well was full.

Murder fucked Brooklyn good for the first round. Upon reaching his climax, he exploded a load deep within her. She then cat crawled to the top portion of the bed, got under the cover, and took her worn out ass to sleep, satisfied with the work her dude put in. He wanted to do the same. But had to stay up to await Jermaine to call back.

***

A Few Hours Later . . .

The time reached 11:30 p.m. Jermaine finally called back with the details to all Murder was seeking to know.

"So, what you find out, bro?" Murder asked.

"I was able to find out damn near everything you had questions about," Jermaine responded.

"Ok. What about the main question? Who the fuck is it behind the hits?" Murder wanted a direct answer.

"Ain't no doubt about it, bro. It was G-Code! He's the one behind it all," Jermaine stated in a frank manner.

"How you so sure on that?"

"Because, nigga, I am! Word is, dude took a trip down to Miami right before the hits started going on. He's got a brother there on his dad's side. The nigga supposed to be G-Code's 'big homie' or some shit like that. He got rank in that Blood Gang shit and put G-Code down with them. All of a sudden, he's Blood now, ain't he?"

"Hell, fuck yeah! I noticed the nigga done started wearing a lot of red now and shit. He keep an ass of them niggaz around him now!"

"That's because Blood protection by the nigga's brother came along with part of the deal that was made while G-Code was down in Miami. G-Code paid a certain amount of money every month. He so happened to put it to his brother that he was in the process of being supplied double the amount of product by some nigga named 'Major.' He's some high-profile nigga who ain't seen too often. A cat that's the number-one guy in line to the connect. He's the top distro. The distro who G-Code normally deal with, referred hm to the other guy, Major."

Jermaine related information that only very few would know about.

How the fuck would this nigga Jermaine know all that if he ain't have a solid source who he's getting information from! Murder thought. *He's definitely telling the truth with all he's saying.*

"I knew it had to be that nigga, bro. I've felt this way all along. But make the connection for me between G-Code and the hitter? What your people saying along those lines?"

Murder urged him to explain the details of the particular point that affected him most. He wanted one hundred percent certainty. There was no room for doubt.

"So, check, right? My source tells me that when dude was down in Miami with the brother, he was introduced to another motherfucka'. A Cuban cat. He had a sister that turned out to be the God honest truth as a hitter. They say the bitch know her way around town real good with a blade. Quiet as it's kept—"

Murder cut in to make a remark. "Yeah, you got that part right! All the hits that's been done did happen with a knife attack. No gun involved nowhere!"

"You see. My people also said G-Code paid the Spanish cat, who had the assassin on his team, a hunnid gees to go around and knock motherfuckas' off he deemed in the way. Say the bitch got a special pair of sneakers she wear on every mission. Like they're a token of good luck or something. A pair of royal blue, high-top red bottoms that has a metal tip over the toe area."

Both of them worded at the same time the description of the sneakers.

"Damn! You all the way on point, bro, with what you're saying. I just never would've thought that nigga G-Code would turn grimy like this and take aim at niggaz above him. To be honest, I practically raised that nigga out here in these streets. And of all people, why the fuck would he cross me out?" Murder vented. "And a hunnid gees, you say?"

"Yep! A hunnid racks. But from how I see it in his mind, he may have figured, why not? You would've never suspected him to be the one behind everything. And especially not slime you. But the nigga a Blood now! That's what they do. Slime niggaz. And stay grimy as they can be. Ain't no love in the streets, Murder. You know that just as well as I do. and it ain't no rules to play by on the way to the top. It's blood sport, nigga! Get that through ya head," Jermaine spat in a cold-hearted tone. Terms that Murder understood well.

"We all got a meeting to attend to in the next two days. I'mma be sure to call out that nigga G-Code there on the spot and make him expose himself. Right there in front of everybody! He may spill the beans on who else in the network was down with the shit he pulled," Murder stated.

"Right, right! One grimy motherfucka' will always try to find another one to link up with. I've got an address for you too on that nigga! Just in case you get impatient before the meeting and decide he's not worthy of being there," Jermaine stated emphatically.

"I know where that nigga at. He over in Jersey. Cherry Hill."

"Oh, that's right. I forgot. Big bro of yours on the blue team," Jermaine responded, referring to the cop brother Murder had.

"Yo, I appreciate you, bro. What I owe you for this?" Murder asked of the incarcerated friend.

"You good, nigga! You don't owe me nothing. Just remember, you do owe me one, a'ight? Now I'm out," Jermaine lastly said to Murder.

"No doubt, homie! One!"

The phone call between the two concluded. Jermaine snickered to himself in the aftermath of the conversation, for whatever his reasons were.

***

Murder went to the living room and took a seat. He had heavy contemplation on exactly what his next move should be. He knew firsthand from experience that if you give a motherfucker a second opportunity to strike at you, they'll definitely take it. And who knows.

The nigga G-Code probably went out and dropped additional money on my head, so he'll be the one a step closer to meeting the connect through Major or C-Ro and if I'm out the way, that'll be better for him, he further thought.

Murder wasn't going to sit back and let his life be taken that easy. Especially if he were able to do something about it. Dude was now ready to suit up and take over matters himself. He felt he had no choice.

***

Two Hours Later . . .

The guy G-Code hadn't long gotten done enjoying a moment of intimacy with a sexy, fit Spanish female he'd recently met. He really loved the way she gave him blow jobs, as oral sex was the only action the two had indulged in. Nothing more. Her reasons for not giving in sexually was that before the passing of her mother, a promise was made that she would practice celibacy and keep her body on reserve until marriage takes place and kids are wanted.

This particular female, no doubt looked good to G-Code. He loved everything about her. They'd been involved only a few weeks, and he couldn't get enough of the kissing and powerful dick sucks she provided.

G-Code was alone in the house. His Spanish companion left an hour earlier, headed back to North Philly from where he was in New Jersey. Before she exited the home, G-Code complimented her on the outstanding dress code she had. She was draped from head-to-toe in Christian Louboutin everything. Literally. But those sneakers she had on. They proved to be the most extraordinary pieces of the entire outfit. They were a pair of high-top red bottoms, royal blue in color, and had a silver plate over the toe area. If nothing else, someone would easily remember them like their life depended upon it.

G-Code was an insomnia addict. He loved to pull all-night episodes. Tonight, he was busy binge-watching *Snowfall*. He had the munchies from the weed he'd smoked. Dude made his way to the kitchen to get a bite to eat. Snack cakes maybe. The refrigerator was his first stop. He wanted a glass of soy milk to go along with the Little Debbie's.

Upon grabbing the milk carton from the fridge, he turned toward the table behind him in preparation to pour up a cup. A shadow appeared in the background. G-Code raised his head to have a look. His eyes didn't deceive him. There stood a hooded figure before his face in his home. The intruder pulled back the cloak of his hoodie to reveal who he was. It became apparent the dark covered man wasn't there at 2:00 a.m. to simply have a conversation.

"What it do, G-Code? How you been? Long time," Murder stated to his former long-time friend and drug network partner.

"Damn, nigga! Wasn't expecting you on such short notice. I thought the meeting was a day or two away," G-Code responded. He already had a strong idea why dude had broken into his place and was there to begin with. And it wasn't to exchange pleasantries.

"It's been a change of plans for you and me," Murder muttered.

"Oh! It has? Well, why don't we talk about it then, huh?" Murder never took his eyes off of G-Code.

In slow format, they both eased the chairs from the table. G-Code took a seat first, then poured his milk. His movement of hands was careful. He didn't want Murder to get the wrong impression, then suddenly start blasting on impulse.

Maybe I can talk my way out of the wrong thought he has of me, G-Code contemplated. *Besides, I ain't done no wrong.*

"So, what brings you here?" G-Code asked.

Murder pulled his pistol, cocked it, then took his seat. There was a silencer attached to the gun he clutched. Gently, he laid the weapon his hand still gripped onto the table.

"I've got all the proof I need, Code. And as bad as I don't wanna do this, I have to. You left me no choice," Murder let out.

"You ain't gotta do a goddamn thing you don't want to, nigga! Other than allow us the opportunity for us to hear one another out," G-Code said. He appeared to be in some type of delusional trance with the way he moved animatedly. Tears welled in his eyes.

"The only thing I wanna know from you, Code, is why bro? Why you ordered those hits on the network? And of all people, why me and my squad?" Murder asked him bluntly. He himself now had tears forming in his eyes. Dude really loved G-Code. Like a brother.

"Why did I order hits on the network and on you and your squad?" he retorted. "How did you come to that conclusion?"

G-Code was still in a trance-like state of being.

"Look, nigga. Here's what I know. Not long ago, you took a trip to Miami, didn't you? You got a brother down there, from what I've been told. How true is this?"

"Nigga! I took a trip to Miami to visit family there! And to get a tan. Yeah, I got a brother down there. Cousins too. How the fuck that make me guilty of putting hits on motherfuckas'!" G-Code spat. He wanted to hear what Murder would now counter with.

"I got it on good authority, Code, that while you were down there, your brother linked you up with a Cuban nigga. A dude who had sure hitters on the team. Word is, you paid the Cuban a hunnid thousand, then put them on a mission to knock off people in our network. So, what you gotta say to that?"

Murder gauged G-Code's energy and body language to try and determine how truthful he would be.

"You say you got it on good authority, right? Who?" G-Code put a serious question to him.

"Humph!" Murder let out in exhale and smirked at G-Code. "Black Jermaine," he declared.

"Black Jermaine!" G-Code retorted. "The nigga that's upstate? One of the most cutthroat niggaz out of Philly the game has ever seen! The same nigga who you ain't never trusted! You mean to tell me that after all this time, and all the bullshit that nigga has put you through, you still believe in him? You can't be for real, Barry!"

"Look me in my eyes, nigga! And tell me straight up like a man. Was it you? Tell me you did it!" Murder demanded of G-Code. The tears now streamed down his face.

He spoke again. "My conscience won't be clear if I know I made a mistake."

G-Code stared Murder square in the eyes. He produced a sorrowful look about the oval-shaped face of his. G-Code's head was slightly cocked to one side, exposing the kinky clusters he had in the mini afro bush of his.

He was willing to answer up to the questions asked of him. "I can't do it, big dawg. I can't admit to something I had nothing to do with. You ain't trying to hear anything I gotta say no how. So, we may as well go on and get to it. We here now at the crossroads. Now tell me something, captain," G-Code stated.

"What's that?" responded Murder.

"After all these years of me keeping it real and being loyal to you, how you gonna take that nigga's word over mine? And what he stand to benefit behind you doing me? Huh? Ask yourself that much."

G-Code was referring to Black Jermaine.

Murder hadn't responded timely. G-Code confirmed. "They say the rain supposed to come down hard tonight. By sunrise. You heard."

"Yeah. I heard. When it rains...it pours, G-Code. And when that happens, somebody's gotta get wet," Murder declared, then rose to his feet from the chair.

Ptui!

He then let off a round from his pistol. G-Code was struck in the forehead.

Ptui!

Another round was fired, hitting G-Code in the chest now. He slowly slumped forward in the chair.

Ptui!

A third round was let off, hitting G-Code in the chest once more, knocking him backwards in the chair to the floor. He was dead as ever.

Murder made his exit from the house. He didn't appear to be in any rush to get back across the bridge to Philly. He wanted to take his time, so as to deeply contemplate over everything once more. After the conversation with G-Code, he wasn't so sure if he'd gotten it right by whacking G-Code. A dude he had love for and brought up in the game under his wing. Murder had a personal hand in grooming the boy for underworld activities.

The reality of the situation was if Murder did get it right, the hits would stop, and there would be no more smoke. But if he hadn't, he'd be forced to deal with a level of regret like never before. He wouldn't be able to back anything. There was no way to bring back anyone from death. In addition to the regret he would have to bear if he'd gotten it wrong about G-Code, the mental agony he'd have to wrestle with would also mean he trusted the words of the wrong man, leaving the money G-Code checked in, the territory he controlled, and the working business relationship the two maintained, would all be up for grabs.

But by who? Who exactly stood to benefit by Murder killing G-Code and getting him out the way? These were the real questions that lingered. Murder may have missed it when G-Code put it to him plain and clear. *"What do he*

(Black Jermaine), stand to benefit by you (Murder) doing me?" Murder shall soon come to know.

To Be Continued . . .

Lock Down Publications and Ca$h Presents
Assisted Publishing Packages

BASIC PACKAGE $499 Editing Cover Design Formatting	UPGRADED PACKAGE $800 Typing Editing Cover Design Formatting
ADVANCE PACKAGE $1,200 Typing Editing Cover Design Formatting Copyright registration Proofreading Upload book to Amazon	LDP SUPREME PACKAGE $1,500 Typing Editing Cover Design Formatting Copyright registration Proofreading Set up Amazon account Upload book to Amazon Advertise on LDP, Amazon and Facebook Page

***Other services available upon request.
Additional charges may apply

Lock Down Publications
P.O. Box 944
Stockbridge, GA 30281-9998
Phone: 470 303-9761

Submission Guideline

Submit the first three chapters of your completed manuscript to ldpsubmissions@gmail.com. In the subject line add **Your Book's Title**. The manuscript must be in a Word Doc file and sent as an attachment. Document should be in Times New Roman, double spaced, and in size 12 font. Also, provide your synopsis and full contact information. If sending multiple submissions, they must each be in a separate email.

Have a story but no way to send it electronically? You can still submit to LDP/Ca$h Presents. Send in the first three chapters, written or typed, of your completed manuscript to:

LDP: Submissions Dept
P.O. Box 944
Stockbridge, GA 30281-9998

DO NOT send original manuscript. Must be a duplicate.
Provide your synopsis and a cover letter containing your full contact information.

Thanks for considering LDP and Ca$h Presents.

NEW RELEASES

SANCTIFIED AND HORNY
by **XTASY**

THE PLUG OF LIL MEXICO 2
by **CHRIS GREEN**

THE BLACK DIAMOND CARTEL
by **SAYNOMORE**

THE BIRTH OF A GANGSTER 3
by **DELMONT PLAYER**

Coming Soon from Lock Down Publications/Ca$h Presents

BLOOD OF A BOSS VI
SHADOWS OF THE GAME II
TRAP BASTARD II
By **Askari**

LOYAL TO THE GAME IV
By **T.J. & Jelissa**

TRUE SAVAGE VIII
MIDNIGHT CARTEL IV
DOPE BOY MAGIC IV
CITY OF KINGZ III
NIGHTMARE ON SILENT AVE II
THE PLUG OF LIL MEXICO II
CLASSIC CITY II
By **Chris Green**

BLAST FOR ME III
A SAVAGE DOPEBOY III
CUTTHROAT MAFIA III
DUFFLE BAG CARTEL VII
HEARTLESS GOON VI
By **Ghost**

A HUSTLER'S DECEIT III
KILL ZONE II
BAE BELONGS TO ME III
TIL DEATH II
By **Aryanna**

KING OF THE TRAP III
By **T.J. Edwards**

GORILLAZ IN THE BAY V
3X KRAZY III
STRAIGHT BEAST MODE III
By **De'Kari**

KINGPIN KILLAZ IV
STREET KINGS III
PAID IN BLOOD III
CARTEL KILLAZ IV
DOPE GODS III
By **Hood Rich**

SINS OF A HUSTLA II
By **ASAD**

YAYO V
BRED IN THE GAME 2
By **S. Allen**

THE STREETS WILL TALK II
By **Yolanda Moore**

SON OF A DOPE FIEND III
HEAVEN GOT A GHETTO III
SKI MASK MONEY III
By **Renta**

LOYALTY AIN'T PROMISED III
By **Keith Williams**

I'M NOTHING WITHOUT HIS LOVE II
SINS OF A THUG II
TO THE THUG I LOVED BEFORE II
IN A HUSTLER I TRUST II
By **Monet Dragun**

QUIET MONEY IV
EXTENDED CLIP III
THUG LIFE IV
By **Trai'Quan**

THE STREETS MADE ME IV
By **Larry D. Wright**

IF YOU CROSS ME ONCE III
ANGEL V
By **Anthony Fields**

THE STREETS WILL NEVER CLOSE IV
By **K'ajji**

HARD AND RUTHLESS III
KILLA KOUNTY IV
By **Khufu**

MONEY GAME III
By **Smoove Dolla**

MURDA WAS THE CASE III
Elijah R. Freeman

AN UNFORESEEN LOVE IV
BABY, I'M WINTERTIME COLD III
By **Meesha**

QUEEN OF THE ZOO III
By **Black Migo**

CONFESSIONS OF A JACKBOY III
By **Nicholas Lock**

JACK BOYS VS DOPE BOYS IV
A GANGSTA'S QUR'AN V
COKE GIRLZ II
COKE BOYS II
LIFE OF A SAVAGE V
CHI'RAQ GANGSTAS V
SOSA GANG III
BRONX SAVAGES II
BODYMORE KINGPINS II
By **Romell Tukes**

KING KILLA II
By **Vincent "Vitto" Holloway**

BETRAYAL OF A THUG III
By **Fre$h**

THE MURDER QUEENS III
By **Michael Gallon**

THE BIRTH OF A GANGSTER III
By **Delmont Player**

TREAL LOVE II
By **Le'Monica Jackson**

FOR THE LOVE OF BLOOD III
By **Jamel Mitchell**

RAN OFF ON DA PLUG II
By **Paper Boi Rari**

HOOD CONSIGLIERE III
By **Keese**

PRETTY GIRLS DO NASTY THINGS II
By **Nicole Goosby**

PROTÉGÉ OF A LEGEND III
LOVE IN THE TRENCHES II
By **Corey Robinson**

IT'S JUST ME AND YOU II
By **Ah'Million**

FOREVER GANGSTA III
By **Adrian Dulan**

GORILLAZ IN THE TRENCHES II
By **SayNoMore**

THE COCAINE PRINCESS VIII
By **King Rio**

CRIME BOSS II
By **Playa Ray**

LOYALTY IS EVERYTHING III
By **Molotti**

HERE TODAY GONE TOMORROW II
By **Fly Rock**

REAL G'S MOVE IN SILENCE II
By **Von Diesel**

GRIMEY WAYS IV
By **Ray Vinci**

Available Now

RESTRAINING ORDER I & II
By **CA$H & Coffee**

LOVE KNOWS NO BOUNDARIES I II & III
By **Coffee**

RAISED AS A GOON I, II, III & IV
BRED BY THE SLUMS I, II, III
BLAST FOR ME I & II
ROTTEN TO THE CORE I II III
A BRONX TALE I, II, III
DUFFLE BAG CARTEL I II III IV V VI
HEARTLESS GOON I II III IV V
A SAVAGE DOPEBOY I II
DRUG LORDS I II III
CUTTHROAT MAFIA I II
KING OF THE TRENCHES
By **Ghost**

LAY IT DOWN I & II
LAST OF A DYING BREED I II
BLOOD STAINS OF A SHOTTA I & II III
By **Jamaica**

LOYAL TO THE GAME I II III
LIFE OF SIN I, II III
By **TJ & Jelissa**

IF LOVING HIM IS WRONG…I & II
LOVE ME EVEN WHEN IT HURTS I II III
By **Jelissa**

BLOODY COMMAS I & II
SKI MASK CARTEL I, II & III
KING OF NEW YORK I II, III IV V
RISE TO POWER I II III
COKE KINGS I II III IV V
BORN HEARTLESS I II III IV
KING OF THE TRAP I II
By **T.J. Edwards**

WHEN THE STREETS CLAP BACK I & II III
THE HEART OF A SAVAGE I II III IV
MONEY MAFIA I II
LOYAL TO THE SOIL I II III
By **Jibril Williams**

A DISTINGUISHED THUG STOLE MY HEART I II &
III
LOVE SHOULDN'T HURT I II III IV
RENEGADE BOYS I II III IV
PAID IN KARMA I II III
SAVAGE STORMS I II III
AN UNFORESEEN LOVE I II III
BABY, I'M WINTERTIME COLD I II
By **Meesha**

A GANGSTER'S CODE I &, II III
A GANGSTER'S SYN I II III
THE SAVAGE LIFE I II III
CHAINED TO THE STREETS I II III
BLOOD ON THE MONEY I II III
A GANGSTA'S PAIN I II III
By **J-Blunt**

PUSH IT TO THE LIMIT
By **Bre' Hayes**

BLOOD OF A BOSS I, II, III, IV, V
SHADOWS OF THE GAME
TRAP BASTARD
By **Askari**

THE STREETS BLEED MURDER I, II & III
THE HEART OF A GANGSTA I II& III
By **Jerry Jackson**

CUM FOR ME I II III IV V VI VII VIII
An **LDP Erotica Collaboration**

BRIDE OF A HUSTLA I II & II
THE FETTI GIRLS I, II& III
CORRUPTED BY A GANGSTA I, II III, IV
BLINDED BY HIS LOVE
THE PRICE YOU PAY FOR LOVE I, II ,III
DOPE GIRL MAGIC I II III
By **Destiny Skai**

WHEN A GOOD GIRL GOES BAD
By **Adrienne**

A GANGSTER'S REVENGE I II III & IV
THE BOSS MAN'S DAUGHTERS I II III IV V
A SAVAGE LOVE I & II
BAE BELONGS TO ME I II
A HUSTLER'S DECEIT I, II, III
WHAT BAD BITCHES DO I, II, III
SOUL OF A MONSTER I II III
KILL ZONE
A DOPE BOY'S QUEEN I II III
TIL DEATH
By **Aryanna**

THE COST OF LOYALTY I II III
By Kweli

A KINGPIN'S AMBITION
A KINGPIN'S AMBITION **II**
I MURDER FOR THE DOUGH
By **Ambitious**

TRUE SAVAGE I II III IV V VI VII
DOPE BOY MAGIC I, II, III
MIDNIGHT CARTEL I II III
CITY OF KINGZ I II
NIGHTMARE ON SILENT AVE
THE PLUG OF LIL MEXICO II
CLASSIC CITY
By **Chris Green**

A DOPEBOY'S PRAYER
By **Eddie "Wolf" Lee**

THE KING CARTEL I, II & III
By **Frank Gresham**

THESE NIGGAS AIN'T LOYAL I, II & III
By **Nikki Tee**

GANGSTA SHYT I II &III
By **CATO**

THE ULTIMATE BETRAYAL
By **Phoenix**

BOSS'N UP I, II & III
By **Royal Nicole**

I LOVE YOU TO DEATH
By **Destiny J**

I RIDE FOR MY HITTA
I STILL RIDE FOR MY HITTA
By **Misty Holt**

LOVE & CHASIN' PAPER
By **Qay Crockett**

TO DIE IN VAIN
SINS OF A HUSTLA
By **ASAD**

BROOKLYN HUSTLAZ
By **Boogsy Morina**

BROOKLYN ON LOCK I & II
By **Sonovia**

GANGSTA CITY
By **Teddy Duke**

A DRUG KING AND HIS DIAMOND I & II III
A DOPEMAN'S RICHES
HER MAN, MINE'S TOO I, II
CASH MONEY HO'S
THE WIFEY I USED TO BE I II
PRETTY GIRLS DO NASTY THINGS
By Nicole Goosby

LIPSTICK KILLAH I, II, III
CRIME OF PASSION I II & III
FRIEND OR FOE I II III
By **Mimi**

TRAPHOUSE KING I II & III
KINGPIN KILLAZ I II III
STREET KINGS I II
PAID IN BLOOD I II
CARTEL KILLAZ I II III
DOPE GODS I II
By **Hood Rich**

STEADY MOBBN' I, II, III
THE STREETS STAINED MY SOUL I II III
By **Marcellus Allen**

WHO SHOT YA I, II, III
SON OF A DOPE FIEND I II
HEAVEN GOT A GHETTO I II
SKI MASK MONEY I II
By **Renta**

GORILLAZ IN THE BAY I II III IV
TEARS OF A GANGSTA I II
3X KRAZY I II
STRAIGHT BEAST MODE I II
By **DE'KARI**

TRIGGADALE I II III
MURDA WAS THE CASE I II
By **Elijah R. Freeman**

THE STREETS ARE CALLING
By **Duquie Wilson**

SLAUGHTER GANG I II III
RUTHLESS HEART I II III
By **Willie Slaughter**

THESE VICIOUS STREETS | PRINCE A. TAUHID

GOD BLESS THE TRAPPERS I, II, III
THESE SCANDALOUS STREETS I, II, III
FEAR MY GANGSTA I, II, III IV, V
THESE STREETS DON'T LOVE NOBODY I, II
BURY ME A G I, II, III, IV, V
A GANGSTA'S EMPIRE I, II, III, IV
THE DOPEMAN'S BODYGAURD I II
THE REALEST KILLAZ I II III
THE LAST OF THE OGS I II III
By **Tranay Adams**

MARRIED TO A BOSS I II III
By **Destiny Skai & Chris Green**

KINGZ OF THE GAME I II III IV V VI VII
CRIME BOSS
By **Playa Ray**

FUK SHYT
By **Blakk Diamond**

DON'T F#CK WITH MY HEART I II
By **Linnea**

ADDICTED TO THE DRAMA I II III
IN THE ARM OF HIS BOSS II
By **Jamila**

YAYO I II III IV
A SHOOTER'S AMBITION I II
BRED IN THE GAME
By **S. Allen**

LOYALTY AIN'T PROMISED I II
By **Keith Williams**

TRAP GOD I II III
RICH $AVAGE I II III
MONEY IN THE GRAVE I II III
By **Martell Troublesome Bolden**

FOREVER GANGSTA I II
GLOCKS ON SATIN SHEETS I II
By **Adrian Dulan**

TOE TAGZ I II III IV
LEVELS TO THIS SHYT I II
IT'S JUST ME AND YOU
By **Ah'Million**

KINGPIN DREAMS I II III
RAN OFF ON DA PLUG
By **Paper Boi Rari**

CONFESSIONS OF A GANGSTA I II III IV
CONFESSIONS OF A JACKBOY I II
By **Nicholas Lock**

I'M NOTHING WITHOUT HIS LOVE
SINS OF A THUG
TO THE THUG I LOVED BEFORE
A GANGSTA SAVED XMAS
IN A HUSTLER I TRUST
By **Monet Dragun**

QUIET MONEY I II III
THUG LIFE I II III
EXTENDED CLIP I II
A GANGSTA'S PARADISE
By **Trai'Quan**

CAUGHT UP IN THE LIFE I II III
THE STREETS NEVER LET GO I II III
By **Robert Baptiste**

NEW TO THE GAME I II III
MONEY, MURDER & MEMORIES I II III
By **Malik D. Rice**

CREAM I II III
THE STREETS WILL TALK
By **Yolanda Moore**

LIFE OF A SAVAGE I II III IV
A GANGSTA'S QUR'AN I II III IV
MURDA SEASON I II III
GANGLAND CARTEL I II III
CHI'RAQ GANGSTAS I II III IV
KILLERS ON ELM STREET I II III
JACK BOYZ N DA BRONX I II III
A DOPEBOY'S DREAM I II III
JACK BOYS VS DOPE BOYS I II III
COKE GIRLZ
COKE BOYS
SOSA GANG I II
BRONX SAVAGES
BODYMORE KINGPINS
By **Romell Tukes**

THE STREETS MADE ME I II III
By **Larry D. Wright**

CONCRETE KILLA I II III
VICIOUS LOYALTY I II III
By **Kingpen**

THE ULTIMATE SACRIFICE I, II, III, IV, V, VI
KHADIFI
IF YOU CROSS ME ONCE I II
ANGEL I II III IV
IN THE BLINK OF AN EYE
By **Anthony Fields**

THE LIFE OF A HOOD STAR
By **Ca$h & Rashia Wilson**

THE STREETS WILL NEVER CLOSE I II III
By **K'ajji**

NIGHTMARES OF A HUSTLA I II III
By **King Dream**

HARD AND RUTHLESS I II
MOB TOWN 251
THE BILLIONAIRE BENTLEYS I II III
REAL G'S MOVE IN SILENCE
By **Von Diesel**

GHOST MOB
By **Stilloan Robinson**

MOB TIES I II III IV V VI
SOUL OF A HUSTLER, HEART OF A KILLER I II
GORILLAZ IN THE TRENCHES
By **SayNoMore**

BODYMORE MURDERLAND I II III
THE BIRTH OF A GANGSTER I II
By **Delmont Player**

FOR THE LOVE OF A BOSS
By **C. D. Blue**

KILLA KOUNTY I II III IV
By Khufu

MOBBED UP I II III IV
THE BRICK MAN I II III IV V
THE COCAINE PRINCESS I II III IV V VI VII
By **King Rio**

MONEY GAME I II
By **Smoove Dolla**

A GANGSTA'S KARMA I II III
By **FLAME**

KING OF THE TRENCHES I II III
By **GHOST & TRANAY ADAMS**

QUEEN OF THE ZOO I II
By **Black Migo**

GRIMEY WAYS I II III
By **Ray Vinci**

XMAS WITH AN ATL SHOOTER
By **Ca$h & Destiny Skai**

KING KILLA
By **Vincent "Vitto" Holloway**

BETRAYAL OF A THUG I II
By **Fre$h**

THE MURDER QUEENS I II
By **Michael Gallon**

TREAL LOVE
By **Le'Monica Jackson**

FOR THE LOVE OF BLOOD I II
By **Jamel Mitchell**

HOOD CONSIGLIERE I II
By **Keese**

PROTÉGÉ OF A LEGEND I II
LOVE IN THE TRENCHES
By **Corey Robinson**

BORN IN THE GRAVE I II III
By **Self Made Tay**

MOAN IN MY MOUTH
By **XTASY**

TORN BETWEEN A GANGSTER AND A
GENTLEMAN
By **J-BLUNT & Miss Kim**

LOYALTY IS EVERYTHING I II
By **Molotti**

HERE TODAY GONE TOMORROW
By **Fly Rock**

PILLOW PRINCESS
By **S. Hawkins**

BOOKS BY LDP'S CEO, CA$H

TRUST IN NO MAN
TRUST IN NO MAN 2
TRUST IN NO MAN 3
BONDED BY BLOOD
SHORTY GOT A THUG
THUGS CRY
THUGS CRY 2
THUGS CRY 3
TRUST NO BITCH
TRUST NO BITCH 2
TRUST NO BITCH 3
TIL MY CASKET DROPS
RESTRAINING ORDER
RESTRAINING ORDER 2
IN LOVE WITH A CONVICT
LIFE OF A HOOD STAR
XMAS WITH AN ATL SHOOTER

www.ingramcontent.com/pod-product-compliance
Lightning Source LLC
Chambersburg PA
CBHW070524260626
47161CB00004B/1633